LOVE IN A

"Parents are rotten," g
you to grow up, then stop
want to because you're a c

"Yes," I agreed. It's easier to agree with Carrie than
to bother arguing.

"Plastic kill-joys that bleep a different language," I
added.

Greg arrived as I started.

"That's a good line," he said. "What's it from?"

"Nothing. I made it up," I muttered.

"She writes poetry," grimaced Carrie as if it was an
illness.

"No kidding! Give us a bit more," he said to spite
her. Greg didn't like Carrie and hated the fact that she
tagged along.

Usually I'm shy about my poetry but I felt obliged
to continue.

> "The creature from outer space
> That works from nine to five;
> Insured for fire and theft and dying
> Yet he's never been alive . . . "

I thought I might as well have saved my breath.

LOVE IN A
DUSTBIN

Janet Green

GOLD
BOOKS

HODDER AND STOUGHTON
LONDON   SYDNEY   AUCKLAND

First published in Great Britain by Hodder & Stoughton 1993.

Typeset by Phoenix Typesetting, Ilkley, West Yorkshire.

British Library C.I.P.

A catalogue record for this book is available from the British Library

ISBN 0-340-58860-8

Printed and bound in Great Britain for Hodder Christian Paperbacks, a division of Hodder and Stoughton Ltd., Mill Road, Dunton Green, Sevenoaks, Kent TN13 2YA. (Editorial Office: 47 Bedford Square, London WC1B 3DP) by Cox & Wyman Ltd, Reading, Berks.

With thanks to

Fay Austin
Katherine Bailey
Hazel Bania
Rachel Black
Suzanne Clark
Samanthea Das
Kelly Dorgan
Emma Edwards
Rosemary Gerrish
Carmel Hope
Barry Hunt
Nanette Jackson
Madeleine Jeffries
Danielle Jones
Joanne O'Shea
Mark Packer
Ken Randall
Simon Stevens
Claire Stiffe
Celia Strange
Dawn Temlett
Margaret Webb
Lynda Whiting

1

"He's on the dole," I said.

"I might have known," Dad muttered, still half reading his paper even though he'd begun the conversation. He shifted in his armchair and mumbled, "Another sponger on the state. He looked like a layabout."

"Well, how old is he then, Sarah?" asked Mum. I realised then that it wasn't a conversation. An inquisition had begun.

"About seventeen," I replied with a shrug. He was nineteen.

I was wishing I'd not told them he was on the dole. I should have said he was an electrician or something. It was too late now.

"You're still only fifteen, Sarah," said Mum, pausing as she prepared tea. "I don't hold with young girls going out with boys that age. He does know you're only fifteen, doesn't he?" He didn't.

"Yes," I replied.

"How long has this been going on?" asked Dad, lowering the paper and giving me more attention than he'd paid me in months.

"A few weeks," I said. That was true. It was three weeks one day exactly.

"Why doesn't he get a job?" asked Dad.

"Be fair, Dad," said Mum. "There's a lot of unemployment around."

Smiling at her gratefully I added, "He does work, sort of. He's got a group. A band."

"Ah. A tax-dodger," said Dad.

"They're only just starting out. They're good though."

"Well, you're not seeing him any more," said Dad with a tone of finality, declaring an end to my romance and an end to the conversation in one breath. Then, as if surprised at his own decisiveness, he justified his decision.

"I've read about these groupie girls. I've read all about them in the papers." I didn't reply because I was choosing the next sentence carefully and, since the silence seemed to require some kind of action, Dad closed his newspaper and folded it in half.

Mum was looking worried. For a moment she had given up all pretence of making the tea.

"You're not a groupie girl, are you, Sarah?" she asked.

"No, Mum."

"Girls that follow bands are groupie girls," said Dad.

"It's a brass band." It was a stupid lie but I couldn't think what else to say.

"That's all right then," said Mum. "You were in the Boys' Brigade Band when I met you, Dad."

"Thanks, Mum," I smiled.

"I was eighteen though," said Mum.

*   *   *

Mum brought the subject up again when Dad had gone to the pub. He wasn't much of a drinker but he liked to pop down to the local for half an hour some nights.

"Just to find out what's happening in the world," he said as usual when he left. Mum smiled in reply as if she was giving permission and then settled down to watch what was happening in the world on the television. I'd finished my homework and I went downstairs to join her.

"Finished your homework?" she asked. The art of conversation was truly dead in our house. She always asked if I had finished my homework and I always replied that I had whether it was true or not.

"There's nothing much on the box," she said. "Let's make some sandwiches for supper." I recognised the

2

situation. Mum always preferred to talk in the kitchen when she had something to say. I followed her with mixed feelings. Experience had taught me not to expect much communication but I did want to talk to somebody and I suppose I was hoping that maybe this time it would be a conversation; the sort of confidences mothers and daughters were supposed to exchange.

Eventually she got round to the first question.

"I've been meaning to ask but it slipped my mind. Where were you when Dad saw you?"

"Outside the chippie." I felt like adding "as you very well know" but she needed all the help she could get.

"What does he look like?"

"Didn't Dad tell you?"

"Well . . . no. He just said he had long hair," she volunteered cautiously.

"He's tall. Dark hair. Long dark hair. Very long dark hair." I didn't mention the yellow streaks.

Somehow I felt she knew there should have been another sentence.

"He's growing a moustache," I added in compensation.

"Have you met his family?"

"No."

"What's his name?"

"Greg," I said. It sounded so ordinary when I said it like that. Just a name.

There was silence while I rolled the name round my tongue wondering where its meaning had gone and Mother stared at the slice of bread she was buttering.

"Are you in love with him?" she asked, buttering the same slice over again in slow motion.

"Desperately!" I wanted to shout but I murmured casually, "It's too soon to know."

She relaxed and looked at me.

"What's he like? As a person?"

"Very nice." He was arrogant, selfish, self-centred and treated me like dirt.

"Does he like you a lot?" she asked.

3

"Dunno."

That was true. He said he loved me. He said I was his girl. He said he'd kill anybody else who looked at me.

"Well, I suppose it's to be expected that you'll be going around with boys," stated Mum. "Don't get too serious too soon, mind."

I couldn't bring myself to answer that so I just shook my head. I didn't need to change the subject. I knew that the conversation was over. There was one thing which needed to be settled.

"What about Dad? He said I wasn't to see Greg again."

"I'll see to your dad," she said. Suddenly I saw my parents and their relationship in a new light.

* * *

I mentioned it to my friend Carrie a few nights later while we were waiting for Greg in the café. Carrie's life is made up of a series of grudges. That night she happened to be off parents.

"Parents are rotten," she grumbled. "They tell you to grow up, then stop you doing the things you want to because you're a child."

"Yes," I agreed. It's easier to agree with Carrie than to bother arguing.

"Plastic kill-joys that bleep a different language," I added.

Greg arrived as I started.

"That's a good line," he said. "What's it from?"

"Nothing. I made it up," I muttered.

"She writes poetry," grimaced Carrie as if it was an illness.

"No kidding! Give us a bit more," he said to spite her. Greg didn't like Carrie and hated the fact that she tagged along.

Usually I'm shy about my poetry but I felt obliged to continue.

4

"The creature from outer space
That works from nine to five;
Insured for fire and theft and dying
Yet he's never been alive . . . "

I thought I might as well have saved my breath. Carrie was straightening her hair and Greg was staring into space tapping his fingers on the red formica top of the table.

"It's not so good after that," I laughed sheepishly. "There's the bit about the plastic kill-joys who bleep a different language and a line: 'Even a computer's got a memory; why can't YOU remember what it's like to be young?' Or something like that . . . "

My voice trailed off and I felt uncomfortable, wishing I'd never begun. It wasn't the embarrassment of reciting in front of them. It was more that I sensed there was no conviction in my voice but I didn't know why. A clear image leapt into my mind of my mum concentrating on a slice of buttered bread and saying, "I'll see to your dad."

A waitress had slopped to the table. She did a deft vanishing trick with our two empty cups as Greg curtly ordered three coffees with a confidence which simply seemed rude. Almost immediately the waitress returned with a sodden cloth and scoured the table top into glistening streaks. I watched her hand and guessed that the others thought I'd stopped because of her. Suddenly I saw my mother's hand. She was always wiping surfaces with a damp cloth. I saw the reddened swollen ridge of flesh on either side of the worn gold wedding ring. I felt guilty. She wasn't meant to be a villain. In a moment of lucidity I said, "It isn't really about parents; it's about teenage rebellion."

"It's good," smiled Greg tapping more insistently. I was startled back into the immediate moment. He HAD been listening. He thought it was good.

"We can use it for lyrics I bet," he said speculatively.

5

"That's fine by me," I said but he'd taken my permission for granted. He turned to look for the waitress. She was enjoying a petty moment of revenge and the delay was making Greg irritable. When the coffee did arrive Greg congratulated her on her speed and efficiency but the sarcasm was lost because her attention was on a table where she thought a tip might have been left.

"Let's move away from the window," said Greg. This was one of his characteristics. He always seemed to think that somewhere else was preferable to the place where he was. As he rose with his cup a man took over the vacant table Greg had indicated. Greg cursed and sat down again.

"We always sit by the window if we can," I said apologetically.

"I like it by the window," said Carrie obstinately.

"That's because you're a voyeur," I joked to diffuse the situation.

"What's that when it's at home?" sniffed Carrie but amiably enough in case it turned out to be a compliment.

"A peeping Tom," laughed Greg. He'd recovered his good humour and mentally I sighed with relief. Then panic caught me again. This was just the sort of moment when Carrie was likely to make a crack about me being top in English. School talk was dangerous. Carrie could be incredibly stupid and Greg still didn't know what year we were in. That first night when he'd taken me into a pub he'd guessed I was seventeen and I'd let him carry on thinking he was right. I suppose part of the reason he thought I was older was the way I talked.

I tried to catch Carrie's eye but she was looking out of the window.

"There's nothing to see anyway; it's dark." Carrie always stated the obvious. It was dark outside; she was right about that but there was something to see, if you looked. The damp pavement was splattered and dimpled with reflected light from shop windows.

It had been raining the night I first met Greg.

"The boyfriend stood you up?" he'd asked.

I'd been round at Carrie's and it was only seven o'clock.

Huddled in the shop doorway wondering whether to make a dash for it and risk my new jacket in the rain, I didn't take in the words. I thought he was asking directions.

"Pardon?"

"The boyfriend. Stood you up, has he?"

Confused and embarrassed I'd muttered that I hadn't got a boyfriend. The slick rain, the splintered pavement reflection, the safe seclusion of the sheltered doorway; it made everything unreal. There was an awning over the shop window, flapping its red and white stripes. From a scurry of wind a rivulet of rain lurched into a sudden trickle.

"Move over! I'm getting wet!"

He leapt into the doorway alongside me and we both started to laugh.

"What's the joke?" Greg and Carrie were staring at me. I realised I must have been smiling.

"Sorry, I was miles away."

"That comes of looking out of windows," said Carrie triumphantly.

I pulled myself to the present and wondered how to turn the conversation back to song lyrics. I wasn't going to miss out on a chance like that if I could help it.

Greg saved me the trouble.

"You need good words nowadays. It's a reaction. Time was when it was all new sounds; but the gear got expensive. There's a swing back to words."

"That's interesting; I hadn't seen it like that." I sounded too enthusiastic, almost breathless, so I paused before I added as casually as possible and with a convincing touch of hesitancy. "You can have a look at my poems if you like."

Inside me, excitement was bubbling up like the froth on cappuccino coffee.

*　　*　　*

A week later I heard my mum and dad talking.

"There! I told you it was a flash in the pan. She hasn't been out all week."

"Well if that's how she behaves with a flash in the pan," said my father dogmatically, "she wants a good talking to. That wasn't just messing about outside the chipshop, you know." There was silence then he obviously felt he had to justify the remark. "I didn't tell you the half of it. His hands were all over her."

"I'll see to it. I'll have a word with her," said Mum.

"If you don't, I will."

I was expecting the follow-up all day but it was the next evening before Mum broached the subject. Dad had gone to the pub and Mum had decided that there was nothing on the box but I had already sensed the interview coming. I was waiting for her in the kitchen.

"How's Greg?"

"Dunno. Haven't seen him all week."

He'd gone off somewhere with his mates.

"Had a quarrel?"

"No. Just don't want to get tied down."

"Do you want a piece of apple pie?"

I could never understand the role food played to my mother. I should have been used to it but the question threw me. It was the last thing I'd expected her to say next.

"It's got sultanas and cinnamon in. And demerara sugar."

I stared at her stupidly then managed to shake my head.

"No thanks." It would have stuck in my throat. I'd hardly eaten all week; I was missing Greg so much.

"Slimming?"

"Yes," I lied.

"It doesn't do to get too thin."

8

"No."

"You haven't been out all week."

I hadn't wanted to leave the house in case he'd phoned. He'd never phoned before but he said he might. He hadn't even sent a card.

"I'm glad you aren't getting involved," said Mum. "Enjoy being young while you can." I detected a wistful note in her voice and I sensed that here was the moment when we might start sharing confidences but I simply muttered, "Yes." My tone seemed like a punctuation mark. It was a full stop. Not just to a sentence but to a whole story.

Mum was buttering more bread than an army could eat. She stared at the slices and said that they would do for tomorrow's sandwiches. Still avoiding my gaze she continued the questions.

"You don't say anything about your other boyfriends."

"There's nothing to say. I don't know that many boys."

"What about the ones in your class?"

I wrinkled my nose. The boys at school seemed so juvenile.

"They're all right, I suppose. We don't mix much."

"Where's Carrie nowadays?"

I'd quarrelled with Carrie. She was my best friend but I often hated her.

"She's gone on holiday with her parents."

For a moment I pondered the stupidity of the lie. It would only need one chance encounter in the supermarket.

"And she's been a bit under the weather," I added but I knew that Mum wasn't really listening.

I sighed with relief but as I stared through the kitchen window I thought of Carrie asking, "What do you see in him? It beats me."

"He's not like anybody I know," I'd answered. That was true. I usually told Carrie the truth, more or less. At least I didn't make things up; I just left things out. But that had been true. He wasn't like anybody I knew. He wrote his own music for one thing. About social injustice

9

usually. Anti-prejudice; anti-war; anti-class barriers. If there was a cause he'd written a song about it. He hadn't got round to anti-sexism yet.

"He's so idealistic," I'd said.

"I see what you mean," Carrie had replied uncertainly. But she didn't.

He questioned all sorts of things I'd never thought of questioning. He talked about the Establishment and left wing politics.

"That's funny," said my mum. "I thought I saw her mother down the shops."

I tried to work out what she was talking about. Luckily she repeated herself.

"I'm sure it was Carrie's mum; this morning. When did they set off?"

"Oh. Carrie, you mean. Er ... I meant her grand-parents. And she's been ill. I was telling you."

I could have kicked myself. Why had I started on the stupid lie anyway?

"Has Carrie any boyfriends?"

"One or two. Nothing serious. She knows Greg. There's a group of us ... " I was making it up now as I went along.

"That must be nice." Was that regret again in her voice?

"It's OK I suppose," I said in a non-committal voice.

There was a silence. There were no more sandwiches to make but she still wasn't looking at me. The kettle and the teapot were awarded her full concentration.

"It doesn't do to get too familiar with these boys."

Mum was getting there at last. I'd nearly forgotten it was coming.

"How do you mean?" I manoeuvred my position so that I looked her straight in the eyes. She looked down.

"They lose their respect for you."

It was my turn to look away. I didn't know whether I was more embarrassed for her or for myself.

"We only lark about."

She seemed to be sighing with relief.

"It's only a bit of fun," I said.

* * *

I went up to bed early. For once I didn't play any cassettes. Music would have hurt too much. I lay there in the dark, thinking. A lyric was running through my head; a love song I'd been working on: "Falling in love is like falling through a black hole into another dimension". I'd started it when being in love had lit up every corner of the day but now I could see the other side of the coin. It really was another dimension; a whole new world; an alien world; and it hurt. I wished I could talk to my mother. I didn't know why I couldn't; she wanted me to. Yet somehow I always ended up lying.

I remembered some advice she'd given me once.

"Be a good listener," she'd said. "Men can't resist that."

She was right. I pondered the matter. Yes, it was a good con trick; it always worked, because of their vanity. The trouble was that I'd despise the men it worked on. You can't build relationships on tricks and games. And where had it got her? She was still listening but he had stopped talking. So that piece of advice was fit only for the wastepaper basket.

I turned over on my bed moodily. No; my mum and I didn't talk the same language; we didn't even think the same language.

My head was playing snippets of conversations like a cracked disc. Now it was Greg talking about Carrie when she'd left us to get her hair cut one day.

"Why do you hang about with that moron?"

"She's my friend," I'd said, frowning. That was true enough. She was my friend. She was still my friend even now when it was one of my days for hating her.

We'd had a squabble about Greg.

"He's too old for you," she'd said. I guessed she was

11

jealous because she hadn't got a boyfriend. The more I thought about it, the more I realised there was another reason. She was jealous because I had been spending so much of my time with him. But she shouldn't have said that. Friends are supposed to stand by you. Friends shouldn't keep on telling you that your boyfriend is too old. Too old. Too old. The words were playing like a backing refrain.

Now it was Mother's voice again.

"What about the ones in your class?"

I didn't like boys my own age. Not since Bobby Cooke. I'd not thought about him for ages but it all came back to me in a flash; a kaleidoscope of impressions. Bobby Cooke with the spiky hair. He used to sing in the choir at church and there was a lump in my throat when he sang, "It came upon the midnight clear." Then his voice broke and he came out in spots. He stopped growing. The last time I went to church I noticed I was two inches taller than him even without my shoes. It never worked out when I tried "Love Friendship Marriage Hate" with our names. I thought I'd solved it by adding our middle names but then I found there was an E at the end of Cooke.

They were always older after that but nothing serious. I fancied my cousin's mate who joined the forces.

"If nobody's got you by the time you're twenty-three, I'll come back and marry you," he'd said. I believed him implicitly and it kept my daydreams going till I met Greg.

I didn't dare let myself think about Greg's past girl-friends; I knew there must have been quite a few.

I remembered that first night in the pub.

"You know, you really turn me on," he'd suddenly blurted out. "I don't know what it is about you."

I felt a warm glow.

"You say that to all the girls," I laughed flirtatiously.

He grinned.

"Yeah," he admitted, "but you'd be surprised how well

12

it works. They want to believe it, you see."

He was talking to me on the level but I still felt let down.

I'd hoped we'd build the relationship so that we'd always talk across to each other. I didn't want to be talked down to; nor looked up to. But already there was a tangle of petty lies.

"You'd be surprised how well it works . . . " I didn't want to think about all those girls he'd tried his patter on; and those he might be trying it on this very minute. I crouched under the duvet. You can close your eyes; you can block up your ears; but how can you keep thoughts from your head?

I heard my mother and father in the next room.

"I had a word with her, Dad."

"About time too."

*   *   *

The next day I saw Carrie in the loos. She was at the sink mopping her eyes. I hesitated then went up to her.

"What's up, Carrie?"

"It's OK, Sarah. It's just that there's trouble at home."

I guessed it was her mum and dad again.

"I don't want to talk about it," she said then told me at length.

"It'll blow over," I consoled her but it seemed to me that a divorce was looming.

"You can't tell I've been crying now, can you?"

"Not really." Her eyes were red and puffy and there were drips of tap water staining her collar.

"Thanks for coming over," she mumbled. "I'm sorry I was a pig about Greg."

"It's OK."

I was glad we were friends. I realised that I'd missed her, the larking about, the laughs.

"How's Greg?" she asked. I knew she was making an effort.

13

"Fine," I said. "No," I added in a burst of honesty. "Not fine. I wish I'd never met him."

Carrie was off boys at the moment; I guess it hurt too much to be off parents.

"Boys; they're all the same," she said. "Boys are rotten. They won't let you shop around till you're sure. They call you a tart if you do. They force you to choose. Then they get fed up and drop you; and go round saying it's because you are a tart. You can't win." She launched into an account of the week's adventures and I never got a chance to talk about Greg.

The next day, however, it was Carrie who mentioned him first.

"I saw Greg in town."

My heart missed a beat.

"Who with?" I tried to sound casual.

"By himself. Lugging a speaker and an amplifier."

"Oh. Did he say anything?"

"He didn't notice me."

"Oh."

It wasn't much of a conversation but I replayed it in my mind all day. So he was back. Why hadn't he rung? Maybe he lost the number. It was in the book. But Simpson is a common name . . .

Carrie went with me to the Grapes. Greg played there sometimes.

"Friday," said the barman.

So Friday we were there

"Hi girls," Greg said.

"You didn't ring."

"I'm here now."

I looked round; there were no other girls in tow.

"Met anybody interesting?" I asked and he understood what I was getting at.

"Would I look at anybody else?" he asked.

That night he was all I could have wished for. He introduced me as his girl. He bought us drinks and cracked jokes. He sang about love and looked at me.

14

I had to be home by ten thirty so I couldn't stay for the last songs but I ran home on air. I'd been carrying my poems around with me for a week and I even forgot to show them to him.

So when did it start to go wrong? When did I start to change?

*   *   *

Autumn came. We were still together. We weren't any closer together. The kissing and the messing about were heavier but we didn't get any closer as people. I grew to understand more about him but I don't think he noticed that he didn't know any more about me. I still hadn't told him my true age – and the longer I left it, the harder it was to tell the truth. My birthday was getting nearer and I was wondering how to deal with that. Carrie's birthday was soon after mine and we were thinking of a joint party but I'd asked her not to mention it to Greg just yet. There had been a lot of other white lies on both sides but they had only been meant to impress and gradually truth sneaked in between the lines. There were moments when I thought that Greg and I were growing to be like one joint person. The strange thing was that the very things which should have brought us together only emphasised my unease. He paid me compliments but I was never sure whether he meant them. I could never decide whether to pay him compliments or not. I feared that if I boosted his ego and made him feel good, he might go off and try to find someone better than me. Yet at the same time I knew that making him feel good might keep him happy to be with me.

My mother had guessed that the relationship was getting more serious. From time to time she asked me, "Are you still going out with what's-his-name?" She knew his name as well as I did.

15

"Um." I tried to make it sound casual, non-committal – but she was no more fooled than I was.

Then one day after the usual sparring round the subject, she asked, "Why don't you bring him home to meet us?"

"I will some time." I never intended bringing him anywhere near.

"When?"

"Some time."

"You're not ashamed of your home, are you?" Those sort of questions really irritated me.

A day later, Dad got in on the act. He had seen a brass band and it had reminded him.

"Isn't it time you brought this lad of yours home?"

"I will some time."

"When?"

"Some time."

"You'd think you were ashamed of him seeing where you live."

I began to think Dad had been taking lessons from Mum.

"He's busy. It's hard to find spare time."

"Busy?! On the dole!"

"He's got a job." That wasn't a lie.

"Miracles will never cease. What is he? Union leader for the dole queue?"

"No," I scowled. "If you must know, he's a male nurse." He was a porter at the hospital.

"Really!" said Mother. I must admit I'd been surprised too. He needed a new synthesiser for the band. He'd stop work when he'd got the money.

"Doesn't it upset you," I'd asked, "seeing all those sick people all day?"

"A load of stiffs?! No. They're usually out cold. I take them to the operating theatre."

"But don't you wonder about them? Who they are? Whether they'll get better?"

He looked at me as if I was mad. I got confused.

16

"It must be interesting," I'd said lamely.

"Now just what's interesting about semi-stiffs on trolleys? It's like stocking up shelves in supermarkets."

"Hospitals are interesting," I'd countered.

"You sound like my old mam. She thinks illnesses are interesting. Varicose veins, piles, the lot."

"It must be interesting for him, working in a hospital," said my mother.

"Yes. Greg does find it interesting," I said.

"Not much of a future," said Dad.

"Sorry he's not a brain surgeon, Dad," I said sarcastically.

"He wouldn't be hanging round with you if he was," said Dad. "Not unless you were a patient."

"That's not nice," rebuked Mum.

"Mind you, he'll have to get his hair cut now," continued Dad.

"I don't know about that," said Mum. "They let them tie it back with ribbons, you know. I saw a picture of a young policeman. He had long hair. So funny it looked under his helmet."

"Well, he's had his hair cut," I said. That was true, only I didn't mention that it was shaved at the sides now and the streaks were purple.

But that had nearly been a real conversation and it was a turning point. They gave me my own key.

"Key of the door and I'm not even eighteen," I joked.

"Yes, I know," said Mother. "Just be sensible."

I WAS sensible about that key. I'd have been a fool not to be.

I knew it was just tactics; my mother had probably been reading an advice column about delinquent daughters. But there was no point bugging them about little things so I made sure I was home early. I knew they waited up for me. I could sense the house listening as I came up the street. There was a sort of obstinacy in my attitude; I was determined not to give them any cause for complaint.

So I was always home early; until that night . . .

17

* * *

"Dad's got to be up at the crack of dawn tomorrow; so we'll be going to bed early. Make sure you don't wake us when you come in."

"I'll be as quiet as the proverbial mouse," I laughed.

"I don't like flippant answers. It's not good in a girl. Where are you off to anyway?"

"Only Carrie's."

"No Greg?"

"No. We're staying in." Lying had become a habit.

"Not taking your cassettes?" You had to give her this: she never missed a trick.

"No. We'll watch TV, I expect," I said, glancing at the paper to check what was on the box in case I got quizzed later.

We were going to the pub. I surreptitiously slid some make-up into my bag on the way out.

Carrie was waiting outside the bus station.

"They've not arrived," she scowled. "I thought it was girls who are always late."

I guessed she was off boys again today.

"No," I said. "Girls are often late; boys just don't show up at all."

"I hope that's a joke," she answered.

"So do I."

But they did show up.

Greg's old banger screeched into the taxi rank parking spaces outside the bus station.

"Get in quick. Don't hang about," said Greg's mate, Tim, leaping out to move the front seat. We clambered in the back.

"Got to call home first. Been working late. Got to get changed."

One of the things that amazed me about Greg was that he lived at home. It didn't fit the image somehow.

"It's cheaper," he used to say with a shrug.

18

His mother was a surprise too – almost the spitting image of my mum. A homely comfortable lady in a homely comfortable house. It was the first time I'd met her.

"Come in, dears; make yourselves at home," she said, drying her hands on her apron and pushing open the front room door. She flurried in to light the gas fire and switch on the television.

Greg threw his coat on the floor, glanced at the paper and flicked the TV over to another channel.

"Football," groaned Carrie to me under her breath. Tim flopped on to the settee. Carrie and I stood uncertainly waiting for someone to suggest where we should sit.

"You'll have to excuse me," said Greg's mum, automatically picking up his jacket to hang in the hall, "I'm having some curtains fitted upstairs. A neighbour's going to sew them for me. Perhaps the girls would like to have a look . . . "

The boys ignored her but we found ourselves bustled up the stairs. Nobody had introduced us so I blurted out our names.

"Well you know who I am; I'm Greg's mum; and this is Mrs Hargreaves from up the street. How are you getting on, dearie?"

Mrs Hargreaves turned on the stool on which she was balancing, a tape measure dangling from her hand.

"Oh good. I could do with another pair of hands."

"The girls will help, I'm sure. I must get back to the washing up. I wasn't expecting them home . . . "

But she didn't leave. Carrie and I measured and chatted, admired the pattern and commented how it matched the room. Though Greg's mother reminded me of my mum I found her easier to talk to and my mind was pondering this curious fact.

"Most places make the curtains up for you but this material was a real bargain on the market so . . . " She paused in mid-sentence and I realised Greg was standing in the doorway.

For a moment I had a spasm of pleasurable thought –
a hazy dream about the future. House. Curtains. All the
things I'd made fun of so often. Greg spoke.

"What's there to eat?"

"You said you wouldn't be coming in. Do you mean
you didn't have dinner in the canteen?"

His mother mentally ransacked the larder.

"I can rustle up a salad . . . I think. There'll be enough
for all of you."

Carrie and I protested that we didn't want anything to
eat.

"A little salad won't hurt you, dears; in fact it will do
you good. You have to keep up your strength."

I volunteered to do the salad; I felt it was the least
we could do. Carrie ended up finishing the measur-
ing and I attacked the lettuce.

"We grow them on the allotment," said Greg's mum,
holding up a pair of socks. I knew she meant the lettuce
but I couldn't help smiling. Yet, if my mother had said
that, I would have rolled my eyes upwards as a gesture of impatience. As it was, I soon felt like cursing.
You could tell they grew the lettuce on the allotment –
complete with a ton of mud and everything that ever
learnt to crawl under the leaves.

"It's very green, growing your own vegetables," I said
politely as I grimaced at a maggot.

I boiled eggs, sliced onions that brought tears to my
eyes, grated carrots and my fingers, cut star-shaped
tomatoes the way I'd learnt at school and gradually
began to enjoy myself. The tin of ham had been kept
in the fridge so it was easy to slice thinly. I buttered a few slices of bread but Greg's mother insisted that the boys would eat far more than that
so I ended up doing the whole loaf. As I saw my
hands automatically buttering, I thought of my mother.
Maybe some day I would tell her about this visit.
Maybe.

Tinned peaches and cream, tablecloth, paper napkins,

the whole works. I was proud of the look of the table when I'd finished.

"Should I brew the tea now?" I asked.

"See if the boys are ready."

"We'll have ours in here," said Greg.

Disguising my disappointment, I carried in two plates of salad with a mountain of bread and went back to see to the tea.

Mrs Hargreaves breezed in to say goodbye and Carrie came down carrying the stool they'd been using. We settled down to our salad just as Greg came in.

"What's for afters?" he queried.

"Have you eaten all that already?" I asked incredulously. It seemed unbelievable that the results of all that effort had disappeared so soon.

After tea, Carrie and I washed up. Greg had changed his clothes and was back in front of the tele.

"Not more football," groaned Carrie.

"Rugby," said Tim, glued to the set.

I sat there watching Greg watching rugby. Suddenly I had another image of the future. I loved Greg but a lifetime of watching Greg watching rugby wasn't what I'd had in mind.

*   *   *

The evening in the pub wasn't up to much either. Carrie and I sat in the corner gossiping. The boys played pool then they played darts against two mates they knew. I couldn't help but remember that first time he'd taken me into a pub. He'd taught me to play darts. We'd giggled and fooled around.

"At least they remembered to get us a drink," grunted Carrie.

Yes, they had remembered. I'd asked for lager and lime and Greg had bought me half a pint. I wouldn't have wanted a full pint but the fact that he assumed girls always have halves annoyed me.

21

Greg and the others came over. One of his mates sat next to me.

"Just watch it," said Greg, "that's mine!"

There was a time when that would have made me feel secure and pleased but that night I felt he was staking his claim on a piece of property.

"Is this the bird who writes your lyrics?"

I'd written a song a few weeks before: "In love with love and not with spotty-faced Bobby". At the last minute I'd changed the name to "Spotty-Faced Jimmy" and it was popular with Greg's band.

Greg turned to me.

"Write us a bit about freedom," he said.

I started to scribble a few basic lines on a beer mat.

"How about," I asked:

"Make, make, make,
Take, take, take,
If you live it up in luxury
Someone else is less than free . . . ?"

"Don't like that," he said.

"I don't reckon much to freedom," I replied. "I think love is more important."

"I don't see the connection," he said. "But write us another love song. You know the score; not a sloppy one. Something with guts."

"Something like . . . 'Love in a Dustbin'," I said off the top of my head.

"Yeah. Don't know what it means – but I like that. You couldn't have a dustbin though. A trash can is better. You have to remember the American market, just in case we hit the big time."

"'Love in a Garbage Disposal Unit'," I said solemnly, tongue in cheek.

"Too wordy," he said.

After they'd gone back for another round of darts, I said

22

to Carrie, "Romeo was sixteen and Juliet was fourteen; I wonder if it would have lasted if they hadn't died."

Carrie was looking disgruntled. She didn't bother to answer. It dawned on me that she'd been hoping for a foursome; Tim and her making up the set. Now, to add insult to injury, the other two mates hadn't noticed her either.

"Read any good books lately?" I asked to break the silence.

I might have known she'd take me literally. Carrie reads love stories. Though I read love poetry, strangely enough I hate love stories. All the way home from school, I often had to suffer the last book that Carrie had read. She'd been into historical romances lately. There was the obligatory fall from the horse at the feet of some dashingly handsome man, usually a highwayman, a few illegitimate babies and heroines who always possessed a long mirror so the author got a chance to describe her. The heroines were usually red-headed. That's probably why I resented them. I have long brown hair; an honest description would be mousey. Carrie had reddish brown hair but somehow boys never saw her as a heroine. Perhaps they read different books.

Carrie had come to life again. She must have been telling me about a book she'd read. She was up to girl gets boy. All the books she likes end up with girl getting boy. The one she was on about at the moment was a historical novel spanning three generations; three generations of girl getting boy.

Carrie hadn't been too happy with that book; too many shawls and clogs. Her tastes were changing. She was beginning to like settings to be modern. I suffered another story. It seemed to me it was just the same – except they met in discos and the mirrors got smaller.

I toyed with the idea of introducing her to some real writers. It would make a change for her. Nobody gets anybody but if they do, they live to regret it.

"They're a good laugh," I explained as part of my

lecture but I didn't bother adding that they always made me feel miserable before the end. Remembering that Carrie enjoyed being miserable I was just about to add that when Greg came back to the table. He hovered over us.

"We're thinking of going on somewhere else after closing time," he said.

Carrie perked up and looked at me excitedly.

"Count me out," I said, "I've got to get home."

"They won't be waiting up. You said so," Carrie protested.

"I know but I don't want to take advantage."

"Well make your mind up, Goody Two Shoes," said Greg.

"Don't mind me." I said to Carrie, "You go if you want to."

"Are you sure?"

"Of course."

It was odd but somehow I knew then what was going to happen. I didn't know what was going to happen to me; I didn't realise then that I hadn't got my door key; but I knew what would happen to Carrie and Greg. I saw the disco as clearly as if I'd got a crystal ball to tell the future.

Outside the pub, we stopped to chatter. Greg was working on an anti-pollution song.

"It's got class," he said, booting his empty crisp packet into the gutter. He stopped to look at himself in a shop window.

"Everything's dispensable to him, even people," I thought. "Everybody's throw-away, disposable."

"I suppose you want me to drive you home," said Greg.

"Don't bother. The bus stop is only at the corner."

Yes, the bus stop was at the corner. I didn't know the buses weren't running after ten that week because of vandals.

*   *   *

It was one o'clock before I arrived home, footsore and aching with my heart leaping at every shadow and every passing stranger.

Then I realised about the key. I turned out my pockets in disbelief and rooted about in the bottom of my hand-bag. No key. I stood outside the house looking at its blank pensive window eyes. Nobody was awake. The house breathed sleep.

I walked up the path. Should I knock? One o'clock. No. I stood in the garden looking at the stars. I placed the Plough, Orion and the Pleiades.

I sat in the middle of the lawn next to the garden gnome and pulled the petals off a sleeping daisy. To knock or not to knock. The last petal fell on knock; but I didn't.

Instead I walked round the back to the lean-to where Dad garaged his car. Access to the car was easy; one window slid sideways with a rubbery chuckle, then I could reach the door handle.

Just then I heard a noise from the house. I crept round to investigate. A light went on upstairs. It was weird seeing the procession of lights, one after the other, room by room. My parents' bedroom, the landing, the stairs, the passage to the front door, then the kitchen with its flickering tube light. Mesmerised, I watched the whole sequence. The house seemed to be holding its breath. Then the process of illumination was reversed until only my parents' light remained staring boldly into the night; then it too was blotted out. Darkness and stillness reigned again.

It hadn't occurred to me to take the opportunity to announce my presence, perhaps because I sensed that it had been my father. My mother would have checked my room. That room had remained in obstinate darkness. It was too late now. I clambered into the car. I spent the night there, curled upon the back seat under the car rug.

I don't remember consciously composing the song Greg had requested, but it was there in my head complete when I woke to the sound of whistling.

It was a high fluting tuneless whistle but from the accompanying clatter I recognised the whistler if not the tune. The milkman.

As soon as he'd gone, I climbed out of the car, leaving it as undisturbed as possible, though for weeks afterwards the very air in it breathed my night's presence, unnoticed except by me. I stood by the side wall with baited breath, listening for the tell-tale sounds of Mother taking in the milk. Late blooming roses cloaked the wall in perfumed shadows and hid me from the world. Dappled in morning sunlight and tasting the clean air, I was almost sorry when I heard the scrape and thud of the bolt on the kitchen door and then my mother's slippers slurping on the step.

The back door would be open. Allow a count to twenty for putting the milk in the fridge. By now, she would be in the bathroom. A gurgle of water rattled in the pipes. Good. Now for it.

Through the back door. So far so good. The foot of the stairs. Hold your breath; here we go. Up the stairs. The blood was throbbing past my ears. Only two steps to the safety of my bedroom.

I made it! Closing my bedroom door, I leaned against it, the panic subsiding.

Now quickly. Rumple the bed. Thump the pillow. Nightdress. Dressing gown. What about my shoes and tights? Where were my slippers? Got them. I caught sight of my face in the dressing table mirror. Make-up! Hand lotion would get it off. Tousle hair. Right. Here we go again.

"Anyone in the bathroom?"

"You're up early, Sarah," came my mother's voice echoing round the bathroom tiles.

"Any chance of a cup of tea?" I asked.

I joined them for early breakfast.

"Couldn't sleep," I said.

"You look washed out," said my mum. Nobody thought to ask what time I'd got in the night before. I was waiting for the question but it never came. I was toying with the

26

idea of telling them the truth. Suddenly I felt that our relationship could stand it. I opened my mouth but Dad spoke first.

"A real restless night I had of it too," he said.

Mum remarked that she had some vague recollection that he'd got out of bed.

"Didn't either of you hear the noise?"

Of course! He meant his night journey round the house. I'd nearly forgotten it. But he hadn't.

Again I was just about to launch into a confession but he took my hesitation as ignorance and continued.

"I'm sure we had an intruder last night," he said.

Mother froze.

"An intruder! You didn't tell me."

"Didn't want to wake you, did I?"

"You mean a burglar?" she asked, clutching the front of her blouse.

"He didn't get a chance to burgle," said Dad smugly.

"You saw him?" asked Mum.

"Well, only in the distance," said Dad gruffly." Big chap he was. Six foot at least. But I scared him off all right."

The story grew even as he was telling it, right to the moment where Dad chased off the intruder with a poker.

"A poker?" said Mum. "We haven't got a poker."

"Oh. Something or other I picked up."

"Shouldn't we phone the police?" asked Mum.

"No need for that," said Dad, coming down to earth, "he won't come back. We don't want a fuss. Best leave it as it is."

I sat there silently staring at my boiled egg. I was as trapped by his lie as he was.

*   *   *

I saw Greg that night. There was a shed where they rehearsed.

"I can't stay long," I said, "I only came to give you the words."

The song fitted the rhythm of one of their present tunes which as yet had no lyrics. While I was explaining this to him, Carrie arrived. She hadn't been at school that day.

"Aren't you well?" I asked.

"Just mogging off," she said and seemed reluctant to meet my eye. I knew then. So my intuition had been right.

Greg was busy fitting up their equipment. He eyed Carrie uneasily then completely ignored her. He sensed I'd caught on.

As soon as Carrie moved away, he said, "You're not upset?"

There was no fencing with words. We didn't have to explain to each other that I knew that he'd been making love to my best friend; and that he knew I knew. It was laughable. At last we were reading each other's minds.

"Upset?" I said calmly. "No. I'm not upset." And it was true.

Strangely enough, I wasn't upset. Not about Greg. As for Carrie and our friendship, I simply felt numb about that as if my brain wouldn't yet face the anger and the hurt.

"You're growing up," Greg said as if he was going to pat me on the back. "People are too possessive; I'm glad we're not like that."

I had a sudden urge to tell him how old Carrie and I were. Perhaps I would say it as I turned to leave. I would enjoy seeing him panic; especially if I said it loud enough for his mates to hear. Already my mind was playing round a new theme for a song – Jail Bait.

"I thought you didn't like her," I said casually.

"Well, you know how it is."

I nodded.

"Relationships have to be fluid," he said. "I feel we're being very mature about this."

"Oh yes," I replied, "very mature."

Tim had been looking at the lyrics I'd written. He came over.

"This is good," he said. "Sounds as if you meant it."

"You're all welcome to it," I said.

I didn't say anything else. I no longer wanted to.

As I walked out of the door for the last time, I could hear Greg beginning to sing . . .

"You got frozen fish fingers
You're a tin of sweet corn
You're a pre-packaged Romeo
You're a book of soft porn.

When you take the wrapper off with loving care . . .
THERE'S NOTHING THERE!

You know what is the essence
Of this tatty love affair?
It's built-in obsolescence
It wasn't made for wear.

When you take the wrapper off; what's the score? . . .
ROTTEN TO THE CORE!

You talk a lot of rubbish
The whole romance was trash
I'm glad we shared the pipe-dreams
But you can keep the ash.

Our love's in the dustbin; what more can be said? . . .
LOVER, DROP DEAD."

2

Your sixteenth birthday should be a big occasion. It should be a time to remember. My whole world seemed to agree about these facts.

"The planning is part of the fun," said Mum anxiously, defensively or indignantly at various stages of catering for the party.

"When I was sixteen our fun was free," grumbled Dad. "This generation don't know how to enjoy themselves without spending money."

"We had such fun when I was sixteen," twittered Aunt Bev who had come to stay for a few days that had become weeks.

"Such fun – wasn't it, Sidney? Or were you too young to remember it?" she asked.

Dad grunted. He didn't listen to her any more than he listened to Mum.

"I'll never forget it; never. We went to the coast and there was a fair," she continued. "Swing boats, candy floss, 'kiss me quick' hats and photos where you stuck your head through a hole. I was Delilah. Now who was Samson? . . . Or was that when I was eighteen?"

Gran could remember being sixteen. Just like yesterday. In fact she could remember it better than yesterday. I suppose all old folk are like that. And she was old. She was nearly forty when my dad was born so she was much older than my other grandmother.

Yes, she could remember being sixteen. During one of my visits to the nursing home, she spent all afternoon telling me every detail of a barn dance and then repeating it over and over again.

"I wore a blue and white gingham dress and had my hair in ringlets. We used to tie them in rags, you know, to get the curl. I danced every dance. Yes, I remember it. I had a blue and white dress, you know."

"So you really enjoyed your sixteenth birthday?" I prompted encouragingly.

She looked at me blankly.

"Are there cream buns for tea?" she asked.

*　　*　　*

At school of course we were always celebrating somebody's sixteenth birthday.

Registration or boring lessons were regularly interrupted by the refrain:

"Sir; it's not an answer to the question, sir; but did you know it's so-and-so's birthday?"

We gave the teachers scores for their reactions.

They got nothing for, "We do not wish to know that."

We could never agree whether allowing us to sing Happy Birthday was a sign of strength or weakness so scoring depended on what happened next. Nervous tics when the singing got too raucous counted less than frantic shushing, arm waving and anxious glances towards neighbouring classrooms. Lusty joining in was acceptable as long as the teacher didn't try to be the conductor. In that case, the class would suddenly stop singing. Top marks came for our history teacher.

"Oh, I hope you have a very happy day and if you remind me at the end of the lesson, we'll all stay behind and sing Happy Birthday to you."

I often wondered if teachers knew that we actually liked them to win.

So, yes, we all knew about sixteenth birthdays being fun and a time to remember. I'm sure that some people in our class prayed that nobody would remember because experience of past years suggested the fun would be at their expense. Getting the bumps with some

31

sadist putting the boot in or being rolled in the sand pit with an icecream cone down your neck is birthday fun to remember for ever.

I was always relieved that my birthday was just before Carrie's because I'm sure that restrained her from the stunts that best friends are supposed to play on each other. But this year, Carrie, my best friend, had already pulled a stunt that eclipsed anything she might do on my birthday. I felt she had betrayed our friendship when she had got involved with Greg. My relationship with him was about to finish but she didn't know that then.

So here I was, planning a birthday party with a girl I despised. Yes, it would be a birthday to remember and if I could get my own back on her I would.

*   *   *

"You've not mentioned Carrie lately," said Mum one evening.

Sometimes I thought she was a mind reader.

"You've not mentioned what's-his-name either," she went on. That confirmed it. I looked at her curiously.

We were in the kitchen washing up and for a moment I nearly told her the truth. Then I remembered that she'd always thought Carrie was a bad influence. I wouldn't give her the satisfaction of saying I told you so.

"I've been too busy with my coursework."

"You're not behind with it, are you? I can finish the washing up."

"No," I answered truthfully for once, smiling to myself at the idea that half an hour saved from washing up could make much difference to anything.

"When I've finished this piece, I've got another to write, about Peace and Conflict."

"That's nice," said Mum.

"I can't start that one till after the school trip to

Coventry Cathedral. That's the week before the party."

I sensed Mum relaxing. She felt she was on home territory.

"Sausage rolls and vol-au-vents," she said. "I think we'll put the table in here."

"Oh it's going to be a buffet then, not a sit-down meal?" asked Auntie Bev, coming into the kitchen and vaguely apologising that she was too late to help wash up. She took a tea towel and dried one cup as a token gesture despite my mum's protestations that we left cups to drain.

"We had a sit-down 'do' last time Sarah had a party," said Mum, "and it was very difficult clearing the tables and chairs for the games."

"Games!" I choked. "What do you mean, 'games'?"

Mum looked non-plussed.

"Well, you had passing the parcel and a treasure hunt. Don't you remember?"

"Yes," agreed Aunt Bev, "that's right; and didn't you do some apple bobbing?"

"So we did," continued Mum. "And Uncle Arthur blindfolded you all in turn for a trick with an eggcup and jelly, something about putting your finger in Nelson's eye. We had the divide pushed back between the two rooms and you had musical chairs . . . "

"Mother!" I protested. "I was twelve then."

"Is it that long ago? My, how time flies."

Looking lost in thought, she dried her hands on the tea towel and murmured, "How silly of me."

Then automatically she looked around the kitchen to see it was tidy and walked through to the lounge. Aunt Bev and I followed in a small procession.

Dad was just folding his newspaper prior to announcing he was popping out for a few moments. He stood up but paused as Mum said, "Well, all the same, a buffet would be easier and cheaper."

"I'm not worried about the cost," I exclaimed.

"I am!" said Dad.

"Sausage rolls and open Danish sandwiches," floundered Mum, "and individual meringue cases."

We were all standing in the lounge looking at each other, uncertain what the conversation was really about.

"A sit-down meal would be awkward," said Mum at last. "I mean, it depends how many people Carrie is bringing. Is her mother coming? And what about her dad? And the brothers? You really should have told us properly, Sarah."

"What's Carrie got to do with it?" asked Dad, though realisation was dawning in his eyes.

"It's a joint party," I said impatiently.

"You mean I'm paying for her sixteenth birthday as well as yours?!"

"It was meant to make things easier," I said, "and you know Carrie can't have a party in their flat."

"And we all went to the circus for their last birthday," added Mum.

"Yes, I paid for that too!" shouted Dad.

"Why don't we all sit down," interrupted Aunt Bev. We obeyed automatically and she continued: "I'll pay for the party. It can be my present to Sarah. It's not often you are sixteen and it's an occasion to remember."

"We're not taking charity," thundered Dad.

"Charity! From your own sister!" Aunt Bev looked suspiciously near to tears.

"Dad, what can you be thinking of?" rebuked Mum, crimson with embarrassment. She looked at him, he looked at Aunt Bev and Aunt Bev looked at the curtains.

"I think we all need a nice cup of tea," said Mum and made her way into the kitchen. Aunt Bev glared at Dad and followed her.

Dad was looking uncomfortable. He picked up his folded paper and stood indecisively. He sighed and sat down again, looking wistfully in the direction of the front door.

"Now look at the trouble you've caused," he said peevishly.

"We didn't want an expensive party," I muttered. "We

34

were just going to have some friends round ... play a few records ... nothing much." My voice trailed off miserably. I lapsed into silence and knew that this was not the time to tell them that parents are expected to go out for the evening.

* * *

"There's a problem about the party," I said to Carrie next morning in registration.

She looked so devastated that I felt protective towards her and confused about my own feelings. I didn't really care whether we had a party or not. Also I wanted to hate Carrie.

I had spent hours thinking how much I hated her. I had planned how I would confront her with the fact that she had betrayed me. But the words never came. Sometimes I sensed that she was going to own up. Sometimes I felt that she wanted to tell me, that she needed to tell me. After all, we'd shared everything till then.

When those moments came, I couldn't help myself. I always reacted in the same way. I switched off and changed the subject. Somehow it mattered to me that things between us should continue as usual, even though I felt resentful.

"Don't you want us to have a party?" asked Carrie almost fearfully.

Again I felt we were verging on the confrontation that I wanted but avoided.

"It's not that," I said hastily and rushed into an explanation. "They thought it would be jelly and paper hats."

Carrie seemed to sigh with relief and life shifted back to normal.

"I can make jelly," she volunteered hopefully.

"No. That's not the point. They thought it was a kids' party and they were going to stay in. They were even going to bring my gran from the nursing home. And Uncle Arthur."

35

Carrie grimaced; she obviously remembered Nelson's eye.

"And they were going to invite your mother," I continued. I nearly added "and your dad" but I wasn't sure whether he was still on the scene. "And your brothers," I added lamely.

Tears were welling up in her eyes but she blinked them away and in the gruff non-committal voice of someone used to coping with disappointment she muttered, "I suppose it's all off then."

I didn't know what to say so I just looked at her. Carrie groped in her school bag for a moment then produced her homework diary. She flipped to the page with the day's timetable and studied it with more than usual interest. Normally she relied on me to tell her what delights were in store for us.

"Another fun day," she commented glumly. "Double Maths to start with. Oh hell; I haven't done the homework. I thought it was after lunch."

Automatically I slid my Maths exercise book over to her. I was in the group above her but the teachers kept the work in parallel so copying was fairly safe.

"Don't go on to the extension work," I said.

Obediently she copied the relevant page but I could sense that she was fretting about the party. As she scribbled I thought back to the carefree days a few weeks ago when we had made such enthusiastic party plans without considering realities such as parents, space, money and vol-au-vents, not to mention Nelson's eye. The days before the silent split between us.

Carrie's biro paused.

"I was beginning to think the party wasn't likely to come off anyway," she said.

"How come?" I asked.

"Just a feeling I had. Remember how a few weeks ago we were deciding what to wear and making lists; tapes to play, people to ask . . . "

She carried on writing.

"Well, the preparations are meant to be part of the fun, according to my mum," I prompted.

"It was more like a game than for real," she said.

"You've copied that down wrong." I pointed to her book.

"I thought I'd better get one wrong or it would look suspicious." She grinned at me but then averted her eyes again.

"And I sort of felt that you weren't so keen on the idea any more."

"Why?" I asked, dreading that she was trying to find a way to tell me about that night with Greg.

"Just things ... I saw Tim in town," she went on casually. "He says Monolith are playing at the Diggers' Arms on Sunday."

Monolith was Greg's new name for his group; he was always changing the name.

"So?" I shrugged non-committally.

"Are you going?"

"Dunno."

It felt like we were skating on thin ice. One wrong word would shatter our relationship. Did I care or didn't I?

"You haven't been round to the shed lately," said Carrie biting her lip. A sudden thought hit me. Had Greg told her that I knew what had happened between them?

I looked away. I wouldn't give her any clues to my feelings. I was going to keep her guessing and take great pleasure from doing so, I insisted to myself. But there was no pleasure. At that moment I knew that I wanted to forget the whole thing.

But Carrie made it difficult to forget. She was like someone playing with an aching tooth.

"Greg asked me where you'd got to."

Something in the atmosphere in the classroom caused me to look towards our tutor's desk.

"Paleface is waiting to call the register," I hissed through my teeth, nudging Carrie.

"They were playing 'Love and Trash' when I went to the shed," she continued.

I nearly corrected the title to "Love in a Dustbin" but I didn't want to upset my tutor by talking. I liked Miss White. She was in her early twenties and she was the only person I always told the truth, partly because I felt she knew it already.

"It's a great song," Carrie went on, oblivious to the fact that hers was the only voice to be heard in the classroom.

"Caroline Johnson," reprimanded Miss White amiably, "I bet you even talk in your sleep."

"Who says she's awake now?" laughed some wise-cracker and the day settled into its usual routine.

"So, are you coming with me to see Monolith on Sunday?" asked Carrie over her shoulder a few minutes later as we battled our way along the corridor.

"Sunday?" I paused thoughtfully in my stride and caused a major collision behind me.

"Oh no I can't on Sunday evening – " saying the first thing that came into my head – "I'm going to church."

* * *

"I thought you didn't go to church any more."

Carrie caught up with me in the upper playground at lunchtime and linked arms. I flinched at the touch but we continued walking, dodging a football.

"No I don't but I thought it might solve the problem of the party."

"You going to pray that your mum and dad will go out for the evening?"

"Fat chance! I just thought we could hire the church hall instead of having the party at our house."

Carrie came to a halt by the litter bin that was being used as a goalpost. Her face lit up and I thought she was going to hug me.

"Brilliant!"

A chorus of football enthusiasts bawled at us to get out of the way. Carrie stuck her tongue out at them and kicked the ball in the opposite direction.

"I'll get you for that, Carrie Johnson," yelled Shane Mackenzie from our class.

"You and whose army?" bawled Carrie as a matter of course and grabbing my arm again she manoeuvred us towards the icecream van which parked by the school gate at lunchtimes.

I paid for two cones and we settled on a grassy slope to watch the duty teacher sneaking round the back of the bike sheds. The look-out had seen him coming and already the refugees from smokers' corner were spilling over into the path of the football players. The air was blue with slanging matches which would develop into scuffles in the corridor in the afternoon and maybe into confrontation at the school gate at the end of the day. Shane Mackenzie was already being told off for his language by the duty teacher who was frustrated at missing his original quarry. Shane knew better than to answer back and he was staring at the ground where a crisp packet blew towards his feet.

"Well, don't just look at it! Pick it up!" demanded the teacher, his forefinger pointing at the offending litter.

"I didn't put it there." Shane had let himself be goaded into replying after all. The footballers were looking on and had stopped all pretence of playing. This was a more interesting game.

"We can use this in our homework," said Carrie, so fascinated that she had let the icecream drip over her fingers. She loved confrontations. I thought at first that she was gloating over Shane's predicament but then I realised her pleasure came from seeing the discomfort of the teacher. To me the whole scene was pathetic though I saw some poetic justice in the class bully having a small taste of his own medicine.

"Homework?" I asked absently.

"Peace and Conflict. You remember, we're supposed to be listing all the conflicts we come across in twenty-four hours."

I'd already listed all the wars going on in the world and had been so depressed I'd given up. But Carrie was right. Paleface had said all the conflicts, big or little.

Carrie was licking her fingers and trying to keep her eyes on the scene in the playground. I looked at her and bet myself that however sorry she was for the victim, she would have been in the front row if we still had public executions. I couldn't help smiling and remembered the affection I felt for her. I wanted to go on hating her but it was difficult. Here was one conflict I couldn't put on my list; the conflict within myself.

The scene in the yard seemed to be frozen in time. The bell went but did not save the situation. Figures came and went in the patterns of students beginning to move back into the buildings but Shane and the duty master remained where they were. We made a token gesture of standing up but icecreams are not to be hurried and dramas not to be missed.

Shane bent down, retrieved the football and tucked it under one arm. He looked straight at the teacher then slowly bent down again and picked up the crisp bag between his finger and thumb.

"He's got style," muttered Carrie and I realised then that she half fancied him.

The master said, "A very sensible move, Shane. Thank-you." Then he added, "It will make up for all the litter you yourself have dropped in the past."

With that he turned on his heel and strode into school, deliberately not turning back.

Shane dropped the crisp packet and booted it into the air. He turned and saw us watching. The aggression corked inside him exploded.

"What you staring at, Carrie Johnson?"

Running towards us, he threw the ball viciously and the remains of Carrie's icecream slurped down her pullover.

"Try to be on time for afternoon registration," said Miss White.

"We had an accident with some icecream," I explained and Carrie looked miserably at the wet patch where we'd tried to wash away the stain.

"My mum will have a fit," she said and our tutor looked sympathetic. She knew as well as I did that money was tight for Carrie's family. Every problem was interpreted in terms of how much things cost. Both her mum and her dad, when he was at home, overreacted because of their financial worries. Sometimes things got violent.

"There's nobody else involved?" queried Miss White. "Not been a little skirmish, has there?"

I looked away. I didn't want to look at her unless I was telling the truth. I sensed Shane Mackenzie watching us. I looked directly at him because I wasn't going to let him think we were scared of him.

"Like I said; we had an accident," I repeated firmly.

"Yes," said Carrie, over-earnestly, "honestly, it was an accident."

*   *   *

Last lesson that day was Religious Education. It was a source of embarrassment to me that I was always top in RE exams and I was somewhat bewildered by the fact. True, I had been brought up to go to the local parish church and I always revised for any exam but I had no deep convictions about the subject.

"You're good at expressing yourself," was the explanation given by Miss White. She taught our class RE but I didn't get the impression that she had much conviction either.

The school reasoned that since the subject was compulsory we might as well all sit the exam. The teachers seemed to be chosen by gaps in their timetables. Mr Lewisham, the Head of Humanities, was in charge but he was known to be an atheist despite the fact that he frequently shouted, "My God!" when people upset him. He refused to take assemblies so we guessed the Head wasn't very fond of him.

Strangely enough, we had very rarely disrupted our RE lessons during our school career, partly out of sympathy with the teachers but also because each of the motley crew had put their individual fingerprint on the course. The Art master taught us all about Islamic calligraphy one term, a Geography teacher was keen on trips and clipboards so we'd walked to every conceivable place of worship while a Drama teacher had done the whole Old Testament by role play. I was Jezebel and we had great fun stoning Naboth with rolled up balls of paper. Miss White was into Personal and Social Education and had a good selection of videos.

"Let's brainstorm," she invited as the lesson commenced. There was a hitch while someone had to clean graffiti from the chalkboard.

"Samantha, come and write the topic in the centre of the board," smiled Miss White. Teachers often chose the girls because they wanted to make sure they were practising equal opportunities. Samantha obviously saw it as victimisation. She never volunteered for anything.

"Go on, Sam," encouraged Carrie out of malice rather than friendship. We'd been talking to Sam earlier and knew she hadn't done the homework. She was a close friend of ours but all's fair in friendship and war.

"You can spell Peace and Conflict, can't you, Samantha?" prompted Miss White but soon added, "Think again about the first word, Samantha."

I was amazed how she kept her patience but I felt irritated at the waste of our time. Soon, however, the lesson was in full flow. A diagram had developed which covered all the sources of conflict we had unearthed in

42

the world in twenty-four hours. Arrows in coloured chalk were making connections. Nobody mentioned the playground at lunchtime but Miss White included "Squabbles among friends" as an afterthought before dividing us into groups. Samantha, Carrie, Shane Mackenzie, a Muslim called Zeesham Hussein and I were working together. Shane and Carrie seemed to have called a truce so we managed to produce a few ideas though Zeesham and I did most of the work and Samantha nursed her private grudge about having to write on the board. We had been asked to think of the reasons behind the wars and the aggression.

"It's Satan and the djinns," said Zeesham pointing his finger at the page where I was busily writing "hatred and betrayal".

"I don't think she wants to know that, Zeesham," I said as Miss White's built-in radar guided her to our table.

"Zeesham has got a point," she said. "There does seem to be a flaw in human nature and in this course we will need to study the theology behind all this. For today, however, we'll keep it simple. A few buzz words we can discuss." She looked over my shoulder at our sheet of paper, nodded and moved on.

"So what are the main causes of conflict?" asked Miss White eventually. We were now using the overhead projector and we knew this was something serious. As each group reported back, some words echoed round the room, a common vocabulary which we seemed to have discovered for ourselves.

As she wrote the words on the transparent sheet we could see her neat printing projected on to the white painted section of the chalkboard. Injustice, inequality, hatred, revenge, fear, jealousy, greed, ignorance, upbringing, prejudice, racism, sexism, class barriers. She added peer pressure and stereotyping.

As the words danced in the glare of the light I knew I wanted to be a teacher. Until that moment I was going to be a journalist and I'd already spent a week of work experience the previous year answering the phones at the local radio station.

Miss White asked us not to write the words down for a moment but simply to look at the list.

"It makes the world seem a sad place," she said finally. Then she gave her customary smile. "But thank goodness that doesn't have to be the end of the story. I'd hate to finish the lesson on this note. I know you've done your homework for this week but I'd like you to think about something before next time."

For once, nobody groaned.

As we copied the words from the screen I was already obeying her request. I was thinking of ways to deal with these sources of conflict. The first step, she said, was making a list of words that meant the opposite. I paused at hate and looked across at Carrie but she was busy batting her eyelashes at Shane who was giving a sheepish grin. Then he nudged her pencil case so it fell to the ground. She slapped his arm. Miss White appeared in front of them, sighed, bent down, retrieved the pencil case and returned it to Carrie.

I stayed behind at the end of the lesson on the pretext of helping put the remaining chairs on the desks. Carrie had a paper round so she'd rushed home.

"Is there something you want to talk about, Sarah?"

Paleface was a silly nickname for her; she glowed with health and life.

"Not really," I said, thinking of Carrie.

"Or just to talk?" she smiled.

Just knowing there was someone to talk to was enough.

*   *   *

I did go to church. Almost the first person I saw was spotty-faced Bobby whom I'd once had a crush on. He was leading the choir and the spots had gone. I wondered what he'd think if I admitted I'd written a song about him. I was glad I'd changed the name to "Spotty-Faced Jimmy". I wondered what ideas people had about me that I would never know.

I looked round at the congregation and smiled at various people I recognised. Aunt Bev was a staunch church-goer. It was as if she felt that being the eldest in the family she had to be correct. She was looking round too and was probably making comparisons with her own church which she had once told me was much "higher" than ours. Our whole family was there. Dad had come to show Aunt Bev that he was a responsible citizen and Mum had come for a variety of reasons including her new hat which Aunt Bev had bought for her birthday to match the coat Dad had given her the money to buy. There aren't many places one can wear a hat. I'd given her a box of chocolates and a book about women in history which she said was very nice and promised to read. The chocolates, however, were very well received. We all dutifully accepted one then encouraged her to eat the rest and enjoyed her pleasure as she worked through the box saying, "Of course, I shouldn't but it is my birthday."

Gran was with us that Sunday for a special visit.

"The family that prays together stays together," she said loudly in a moment of lucidity but unfortunately in the middle of the sermon.

"Hush!" said Aunt Bev.

"Doesn't the vicar look young," said Gran even louder. "It's the same with policemen."

"I saw a photo of a policeman with long hair under his helmet," whispered Mum helpfully.

"For God's sake, don't encourage her," said Dad and Mum, reprimanded, fell silent.

Aunt Bev passed peppermints along the row as if it was part of the religious ritual and we all surreptitiously sucked them. Gran was fiddling with a peppermint stuck in her teeth and asking if we'd remembered to get her a bottle of Guinness.

"The nursing home lets me have one. It's good for you."
I was about to get the giggles.

"Let us pray for peace in the world."

The words riveted me. I swallowed the mint, forgot Gran and lost the urge to giggle because suddenly I wanted to be part of this moment. I wanted to pray for peace in the world. I closed my eyes and saw the list on the overhead projector screen, the chalkboard with the conflicts in the world, the words "squabbles among friends" and superimposed on the kaleidoscope of images I saw the face of Carrie.

*　　*　　*

Eucharist was at the end of the service. I had been confirmed so I could have joined in but it was obvious that the rest of our group was wanting to go.

"Are you ready, Sarah?" asked Mum as if she sensed my hesitation. "The roast is on the pre-timer. Perhaps I should have stayed home."

"No, I'm glad you came. I'm fine. I'll give you a hand with dinner. That's what daughters are for," I laughed. Helping with dinner was the least I could do and I wanted Mum to know that I did care.

Aunt Bev was pulling on her gloves in the church porch with a self-satisfied smile.

"Well, Sarah. That's that. Now we've been to the service we'll be able to ask the vicar about the church hall. Your idea about using it was admirable. You seem to be a sensible girl. I don't know where you get it from. And if we are going to do things properly perhaps we should have outside caterers."

Anxiously I turned to check that Mum hadn't heard.

"No. Thankyou all the same, Aunt Bev; but the preparations are part of the fun."

"That's all very well for you to say, my girl. Perhaps you're not so sensible after all. Think of all the work for your poor mother."

46

I wanted to shout, "I'm not your girl and I'm being sensitive not sensible," but I merely smiled pleasantly.

"Carrie and I will be helping her and we'll enjoy it." This time my smile was genuine as I pictured Carrie's face when she heard this latest piece of news.

*   *   *

"You mean she was going to pay for outside caterers?"

Carrie couldn't get over it.

She had greeted the fact that she and I would help with more enthusiasm than I'd anticipated but she couldn't get over the idea that we nearly had outside caterers.

"It's going to be fun helping your mum. She does good parties, you know."

"Yes, I know."

"My mum said she's working but she would make some jellies for me to bring. I told her jellies weren't a good idea and she said she'd do some trifles. Sherry trifles."

We sat on the grassy slope in our usual lunchtime haunt even though November weather made the grass damp.

"I'm glad I'll be able to help. It'll feel more like my party too."

The grass seemed to slip under me. Why had I never realised how she felt when my family took charge?

"Outside caterers! Is she rich, your Aunt Bev?"

"Not by rich people's standards but she's better off than we are. She's Dad's oldest sister. He's got two others but we hardly ever see them. Her husband died and she's got a pension from where he worked. She has a son in Australia who seems to be doing well in real estate and a daughter in Canada. But they never come over here."

"I wish I had relatives like that," said Carrie.

"What? Far away?" I laughed.

47

"No; with money."

"Money's not everything," I answered, "and Aunt Bev's not had it easy. Her other son was killed in the Gulf War." An image of Richard leapt into my head, laughingly calling me his little cousin. I'd hero-worshipped him.

"Oh, I remember that. You were really cut up about it. You were the first person I knew who'd been to a funeral."

I glanced at her, half expecting a ghoulish look but all I saw was sympathy.

"That's when I stopped going to church," I said.

Carrie didn't ask any more questions but fumbled in her pocket.

"I've got some chewing gum. Want some?" She offered the piece awkwardly.

"It's your last piece."

"That's OK. I'd rather you had it."

I accepted it wondering when she would ever remember that I don't like chewing gum.

Shane Mackenzie appeared, holding a football.

"What's that you're giving away?"

"Gum. I haven't any more; sorry."

He flopped down on the grass next to Carrie but when he was convinced she was telling the truth he stood up again.

"Don't forget to be early on Friday, Carrie," he said, "we want to get the back seat on the coach."

"So, you've got a date for the Coventry trip," I grinned when he'd gone. "I thought you said anybody who looked at him twice needed their eyes testing," I added, "and a brain transplant."

"Anybody can change their mind; it's a free country," she sniffed amiably.

I could tell she was pleased about Shane but she didn't seem as enthusiastic as I'd expected.

"We haven't got him on the list. Are we inviting him to the party?" I asked with some misgivings.

"Naw. He's just a kid; a bit of fun. I've got bigger fish to fry."

I wondered if she meant Greg. An image of him came into my mind and I was amazed that it provoked no feelings at all. Yet a few months ago I would have sworn that this was the big love affair of my life. Now it was in the dustbin.

Carrie and I still hadn't talked about Greg. I decided that I ought to make it plain that as far as I was concerned my relationship with Greg was over and she was welcome to him.

"Did you go to see Monolith?" I asked.

"Didn't I say?" she replied, knowing very well that she hadn't. "It was a great night. You should have come."

"It's all over between Greg and me, you know."

"I guessed," she said simply, "but that shouldn't stop you seeing them play. I was chatting to Tim and he says he hopes you'll carry on writing for them."

I felt a thrill of pleasure but didn't know what to say next. We were each stepping very carefully in this conversation and I was having difficulty interpreting the real meanings.

"Are we going to have tapes at the party?" Carrie asked suddenly. "I was wondering if we should ask Monolith. I mean, we're not having real caterers but we could have a live band. There's a stage in the church hall, isn't there? And if I set it up it could be my contribution to the party."

A sudden suspicion crossed my mind.

"Have you told Greg about the party?" I asked.

"No." Something in her tone told me not to believe her but I didn't say anything.

She paused, seemed to come to a decision and said, "I told Tim. I haven't asked them to play or anything."

"Did you tell him it's a sixteenth birthday party?" I asked curiously.

"No," she said impatiently, "you've been telling me for months that they thought we were seventeen."

"Well, they'll soon know if they come to the party," I said.

* * *

Miss White was ticking off the names at the door of the coach as each person boarded.

Carrie and I were halfway down the aisle in hot pursuit of Shane who was making for the prime seats in the back row. My jacket caught on the arm of a seat and the moment's delay gave half a dozen contestants the opportunity to push past.

"Don't shove!" I protested and saw Carrie waving wildly and trying vainly to spread her bulk to save two seats. A free-for-all was developing.

Miss White leapt into action. She forbade anyone else to get on the coach, boarded it herself and bellowed for silence.

"Off!" she demanded. Sullenly, nursing our gear, we trooped back down the aisle and off the bus. "I tried to treat you like human beings," she shouted after us in exasperation.

She stood in the doorway looking down at us.

"Line up sensibly and when you enter the bus start filling it up from the front; two seats at a time, first the left pair of seats and then the pair on the right. And remember, if you can't do it sensibly, we'll have a practice drill at the end of the day."

Shane and Carrie were already jockeying for positions at the end of the queue which would leave them in the back seats. I didn't really care. I preferred to sit near the middle and I didn't honestly want to get involved in any stupidity in the back row.

Miss White had to start ticking off the names again. It occurred to me that because she was so young she probably didn't have much experience of school trips. When she was at school, I bet she didn't make a beeline for the back row. I wondered if she sat at the front in the classrooms too. I would have liked to sit in the front row in lessons but Carrie always steered me to the back.

Miss White paused. She noticed Shane staking his claim at the end of the queue. Only two people had got on the bus so far.

"Shane, come to the front of the queue, please; you can get on now."

"She learns fast," I thought. Carrie had sidled from the back and made a space for herself behind me. She was counting the heads to make sure we would end up sitting together.

There were ninety of us going on the trip so we needed two coaches. The rest of the year were going the following week.

The coach behind ours was being organised by Mr Lewisham and, though he had managed to get the students on the coach, he was having problems of his own. A large bottle of pop had burst open when somebody dropped a bag. Mr Lewisham was trying to usher the owner of the offending bottle down the steps back into the street. The embarrassed student was clutching the bottle to his chest in blind panic and the contents were spraying out in a soda siphon stream of fizzy orange. Our queue fell about laughing and some of those on the coach rushed back down to see the fun.

*   *   *

At last we were off. There were three teachers on our coach. Miss White and the new young Art master Mr Pickering (already christened Picasso) sat near the back where there were still spaces. The third teacher was old Mr Singleton who taught Maths but seemed more interested in counting the days to his retirement. He insisted on sitting at the front of the coach. This involved moving someone to make a vacant place. Shane volunteered and gleefully rushed down the bus to settle in solitary splendour in the middle of the back row.

51

The journey was fairly uneventful except for a continuing wrangle with the coach driver. He reluctantly gave in to Miss White when she asked him to play our tapes but got his own back by turning down the volume. We didn't stop at the service station on the motorway on the grounds that we had already delayed too long but I suspected it was because the staff couldn't face the chaos of getting us all off and on the coaches again. It was a two-hour journey but the coach driver spent an extra twenty minutes driving round a one-way system trying to locate the entrance to the cathedral. By then, someone had been sick in a brown paper bag and half a dozen were crossing their legs and wailing that they couldn't wait.

The staff weren't sure of the route but Zeesham had relatives in Coventry and he eventually went to the front to direct the driver to the cathedral. It was about this time that Miss White noticed a wisp of smoke floating down the aisle and caught the whiff of tobacco in the air. We'd noticed it earlier.

"Somebody's playing with fire," Carrie whispered with unconscious wit.

As our coach pulled up before the steps of Coventry Cathedral, Picasso was conducting an investigation. We could hear the clatter of him prying into the ashtrays at the back. He couldn't prove his suspicions but I noticed he sat in the back row next to Shane on the return journey.

Miss White placed a huge black plastic rubbish sack at the front of the coach.

"Crisp bags, toffee papers, empty cans, all your litter, please – in the bag," she announced over the driver's microphone. From the look on her face, I felt she would gladly have deposited some of us in there too. "Don't move from your places yet. There are one or two things I need to say."

"Aw, miss. Hurry up, miss. I'm dying," came a plaintive plea from Sam behind us.

We were instructed to be certain that we could recognise our coach and the driver. He turned round to scowl at us. We'd remember him all right. First, we were to assemble on the steps by the statue of St Michael and the Devil, said Miss White. The teachers would escort small groups to the toilets and we would then receive our timetables for the tour.

"Finally, a school trip is meant to be enjoyed but do remember this is a cathedral."

Miss White was pink and getting flustered at the growing impatient fidgeting on the coach.

"We'll check your names and put you in groups while you're still under the Devil; that's him with the horns."

"I thought that was Mr Lewisham," said some wisecracker, seeing the other coachload already assembling at the appointed place.

"Oh no; that's Satan," said Zeesham with enthusiasm, leading our troops out of the bus in the wake of the Maths master.

Miss White remained behind to check for litter and consult with the driver about the time of departure.

I'd seen pictures of the cathedral and I'd paid attention in class when Miss White prepared us for the visit but the reality overwhelmed me. The stark dramatic outline of the war-damaged ruins and the gleaming façade of the modern cathedral were such a contrast and yet seemed totally in harmony.

"It's not like a cathedral," said Carrie as we walked up the steps. "And that bit over there looks like somebody dropped a bomb on it."

*   *   *

We were in our three teaching groups, each of about thirty students with two teachers. Our group had Paleface and Picasso.

"Remember," said Mr Lewisham to all of us before the groups went their separate routes, "wherever you are just

53

before twelve noon, you must make your way to the altar in the ruins."

"Or you'll turn into a pumpkin," muttered Carrie.

"Why can't we all go in one big group, sir?" asked Samantha, whose boyfriend, Paul, was in the other class.

Mr Lewisham gave her a withering look then ignored her. His group set off towards the visitors' centre. We remained under the canopy which linked the old and the new cathedrals and Sam gazed forlornly after the retreating figure of Paul. Carrie nudged me and indicated we should go and stand with Sam. It seemed a kindly thought but you could never be sure with Carrie; she often fussed like a mother hen when other girls were showing signs of distress but ended up stirring more trouble than there was in the first place.

"I hate that Mr Lewisham," said Sam.

"It was nothing personal," I said. "He's only doing his job."

"Well, he might do it with more feeling," said Carrie petulantly. Sam gave her a grateful smile.

Our group's tour began at the great east window. We gaped up at the etchings from the outside. I was conscious of the reflection of the ruins behind us with the shadows staining us and the area in which we were standing.

From the inside, we could see the ruins looming beyond and it was clear that we were meant never to forget their presence. A cathedral guide had joined us and he was explaining who the saints were on various rows but to me they were insignificant. It was the rows of angels leaping in weird contortions that caught my imagination. Zeesham was standing next to me.

"I like angels," he said. "We greet our own two angels at the end of our prayers. One on our left shoulder and one on our right." I looked at him as if I was seeing him for the first time and wondered about his beliefs. My mother often remarked about guardian angels but I'd never met anybody else who took them seriously.

"That one in the middle looks spastic to me," said Carrie. I glared at her and said, "He's jumping for joy."

The guide told us that the engraver died from the dust caused by his job. Our group grew silent. A few started to make notes on the sheets in their clipboards.

The atmosphere was nearly ruined by a lady who came over to complain about somebody taking photographs but it turned out that the school had paid for the privilege.

"It's only so we'll buy their postcards that they stop us taking photos," said Shane cynically.

"That's Christians for you," sniffed Carrie.

"We're going to the Chapel of Unity next," said Miss White but Shane had got there first. He was hopping around the mosaics on the floor. The guide managed not to show his annoyance and said the floor of the circular room had been a gift from Sweden. There were beautiful symbols for the continents round the edges of the floor and a dove in the centre. The guide produced some marbles and asked people near the continents to place the marbles there. We watched, mesmerised, as the marbles slowly began to roll towards the centre. The guide explained that this was symbolic of unity. Then he pointed to a large black wooden cross suspended above.

"The cross will be painted white when there is peace throughout the world."

There was silence. The slump of all our shoulders suggested that none of us had much hope of the painter being called in.

Outside the chapel, we paused by a sculpture of the head of Christ crucified.

"Helen Jennings made that for someone whose son died in a car crash," said Miss White, taking over from the guide who had merely drawn our attention to it, saying it was made from the metal of wrecked vehicles.

"What do you think was in her mind?" asked Miss White.

Immediately the face of my cousin came to my thoughts but I didn't say anything.

"I like to think," continued Miss White when nobody responded, "that she was letting out the anger and the hate and making something beautiful that would help other people cope with their pain and their sorrow."

Then we stood under the glorious colours of John Piper's baptistery window. I recognised it from our textbooks and I heard the guide telling us that the rough-hewn font underneath was a boulder brought from Bethlehem but I wasn't really listening. I had fallen in love with a window.

"It's God's love bursting into the lives of individuals," said Miss White. I looked at her curiously and began to revise my ideas about her beliefs.

As we moved on we could already see the famous tapestry by Graham Sutherland of Christ in glory and I understood why it had been so controversial. The swirl of the robes made it look like a huge cocoon and I decided that I didn't like it.

The guide began to explain the symbolism of the windows we were passing which were meant to signify the changing stages of life. The windows were at a strange angle and you couldn't appreciate them until you had reached the end of the sequence. Carrie and I happened to be standing near Shane and Miss White.

"The colours are nice, miss," said Carrie. She was quite fond of Paleface.

"Yes, but I must admit I prefer conventional church windows. It seems so odd to me that these have no impact until you reach this vantage point."

"That's like life, ain't it?" interrupted Shane. "It's only when you get past something that you start to understand it." He wandered on ahead of us leaving Carrie, me and Miss White gaping, open-mouthed.

The group assembled by a metal grid of thorns through which we could see the Chapel of Gethsemane.

"Get that!" said Shane enthusiastically. The guide was explaining that the chapel was constructed so natural light fell on the golden angel holding the cup of suffering. Zeesham was clutching the metal frame of thorns, fascinated by the gleaming mosaic of the angel.

"Look, the disciples are asleep," he said.

The others had moved on. Zeesham and I hurried into the next chapel in time to hear Miss White say, "People often think the church and the world are separate; so why do you think the windows, here, let you see the world outside?"

"It's not much of a view," commented Sam.

"But it's Coventry, an industrial city; and this is their cathedral," answered Miss White.

"You mean people have services here?" asked Carrie and everybody started to giggle.

Miss White smiled and replied tactfully, "It's easy to forget that when you're looking at all the works of art and the gifts from around the world."

Eventually we returned to the tapestry. It was huge.

"It's not painted," I explained to Carrie who seemed to see it as a theatrical backcloth, "It's woven."

I didn't like the tapestry but somehow it haunted me.

"The eyes seem to follow you," said Carrie.

"That's a cheap trick," I was going to say but I didn't want to dampen her enthusiasm.

"We'll see the original sketches for the tapestry when we go to the visitors' centre," said the guide.

"Those are the four evangelists in the corners," he went on.

"What's he talking about?" muttered Carrie.

"The gospel writers. Those are their symbols. The eagle is John."

"Eagle? What eagle? It looks like a parrot to me."

She was diverted by the guide directing our attention to the altar cross.

"In the centre you can see the cross of nails."

Miss White had made a big thing about the Community of the Cross of Nails in our lessons so our pens were flying across the notepads as the guide explained that it was an international symbol of reconciliation.

"It's made from three medieval nails which were found among the debris after the bombing," he said, leading us

57

back down the church to the exit. He pointed out the pennies set in the floor to guide the choristers and we all solemnly trooped from penny to penny behind him.

*   *   *

The film we saw in the visitors' centre was fantastic. Miss White and Picasso were obviously worried about any situation where the lights would be turned off but they needn't have bothered. We were positively angelic apart from somebody who was blowing bubble gum that popped all over his face.

We shared the viewing area with some Japanese and German tourists. The moment which stayed in my mind was the sight of the rubble in the bleak November morning after the bombing and the commentator explaining how Jock Forbes had found two burnt beams fallen in the shape of a cross, the symbol of suffering. The view was from the stone tower which had remained intact and you could see the beams almost central in the ruins. I could imagine how those people felt, walking among the smouldering embers. Yet they chose forgiveness not revenge. The film showed the devastation of German cities like Dresden. I looked curiously across at the German tourists and wondered what they were thinking. The forgiveness needed to work both ways. But then, the very fact that they were here in Coventry said a lot about this group.

I felt mind-blown as I came out of the viewing area. The feeling was reinforced by that odd sensation of coming out of a film into the daylight.

"We won't have time to go up the tower now," said Miss White, "so I'm going to take you very quickly round the rest of the visitors' centre. The tower will have to be after lunch and it will be optional."

I tagged along with the others looking at the tapestry sketches but my thoughts were still in the viewing room. I began to concentrate more when we stopped in front of the actual charred cross.

"What's that in the ruins then?" somebody asked.

"That's a fibreglass copy. This one was gradually suffering from the weather and the pollution," explained the guide, then added, "and unfortunately from graffiti and souvenir hunters." I looked at the charred cross sadly and began to think about the crucifixion; it seemed to me that it was still going on.

* * *

It was noon. We were all assembled in the ruins, our attention focused on the altar, and behind it, the copy of the burnt cross. The words engraved on the altar were, "Father Forgive".

We already knew that this service happened every Friday and that was why our trips had to be on that day.

There were about two hundred people of many different nationalities but we were the largest single group. I saw Samantha standing next to Paul and I smiled.

The clergyman leading the short service said he would ask one of the congregation to lead the prayer. He looked round and his gaze fastened on Shane. I couldn't resist looking at Miss White. I could imagine the thoughts in her head. Shane could read quite well but he would probably have been her last choice if she'd been asked. Mr Lewisham was looking up to the sky as if praying for a miracle and Picasso was grinning.

Shane ambled forward. He studied the card handed to him and then started leading us in prayer. At regular intervals we had to join in the words, "Father Forgive."

Shane looked round as if to make sure we all had our eyes closed and I noticed one or two of his cronies pulling faces at him. He ignored them and I closed my eyes to say a quick prayer for him before he began.

"Father forgive
the hatred which divides nation from nation, race from race, class from class,

Father forgive
the covetous desires of men and nations to possess
what is not their own,
Father forgive
the greed which exploits the labours of men and lays
waste the earth . . . "

Eventually he reached the final "Father Forgive". He heaved a sigh of relief and so did Miss White.

Shane handed the card back to the Provost and moved forward to rejoin our group. I was expecting a smirk of triumph or pride but as he passed me I noticed a glimmer like tears in his eyes. I saw Miss White was also watching him. She smiled and there were tears in her eyes too.

*   *   *

"Fifty-four, fifty-five, fifty-six."

We were staggering up the tower with our lunch heavy inside us and Carrie was behind me counting the steps.

To the surprise of Paleface and Picasso, all our group had decided to join in except a few who were afraid of heights and Zeesham who had got permission to go back to look at the angels. I had been surprised too, knowing that a journey up the tower would erode some of our precious free time and remembering how keen Shane and Carrie were to slip away from our gaolers. Paleface had stayed with the invalids in the souvenir shop and Picasso was leading the expedition. Then it occurred to me that maybe the attraction was the opportunity to bait the Art master. With innocence and enthusiasm he was encouraging us to put our best foot forward.

"Which one's that, sir?"

Sam's voice carried down the stairs towards us. She was in a good mood because Paul had been allowed to join our group. They were trying to go up the stairs with their arms round each other.

Carrie came to a halt.

"Stop that, Shane! You go in front of me!"

"I'm not having him behind me," I complained.

Shane protested his innocence but obligingly squashed past the two of us and went on ahead. I paused to nurse my foot.

"You clumsy idiot," I growled.

"I've just washed my feet and I can't do a thing with them," he laughed then cursed as he tripped over a step.

"What number was I up to?" asked Carrie.

"How should I know?"

"Never mind; I'll count them on the way down. What are we doing this for, anyway? It's murder on my knees."

"Well, walk on your feet then," shouted Shane.

"I want to see the view," I said.

"I suppose it's good exercise," Carrie puffed.

"And we'll be able to tell everyone we got to the top," I said to encourage her.

"If we live to tell the tale!" she groaned.

"But what a way to spend my birthday," I laughed.

"And it's only one week and one day till the party. I can't wait!" she said, cheering up.

She chanted "Party! Party!" for the next few steps until Shane called from above, "What party?"

"The monster raving loony party!" she bawled back and the words reverberated around the walls.

"We haven't sung 'Happy Birthday To You' yet." I'd been hoping she'd forgotten that; I'd got off very lightly this birthday.

"Happy Birthday to you," she began singing then shouted up the staircase, "Hey, everybody, it's Sarah's birthday today."

So twenty-odd of them plodded up the steps singing, "Happy Birthday to you."

Picasso was having a fit at the top as the acoustics bombarded him with echoes but he was helpless; there was nothing he could do to stop them. "Shut up!" he bawled, the words bouncing from wall to wall. This

61

merely inspired someone to start on "She'll be coming up the mountain when she comes."

At the top we each had a lecture about behaviour as we emerged into the light. The view across the city was great. I breathed the November air and looked down at the scarred shell of the old cathedral, thinking of that other November and the charred cross.

"Oooh! I feel dizzy," said Carrie at my elbow.

"Well, don't look down then."

"I won't be able to see anything if I don't look."

"There's a McDonald's," said Shane. "I reckon we could make it there and back after this."

Picasso overheard him.

"The free time is for buying some souvenirs and finishing your coursework notes."

"And for you to have a coffee," grinned Carrie.

"You're not to leave the compound," he said as sternly as he could and turned to a more studious group who were asking if they could look at the bells on the way down.

"The Bells! The Bells!" said Shane, doing a hunchback of Notre Dame round to the other side of the roof area.

Picasso decided it was time to return and began to shepherd us towards the stairs. He started counting us through the door but a Japanese gentleman was coming up and his camera strap got entangled with somebody's clipboard. Picasso lost count, ushered Carrie and me in front of him and we began the descent. Carrie wailed that she'd forgotten to count the stairs.

We were at the bottom when it became clear that we were one student short. Shane was missing.

"If you're going back up, sir, will you count the steps for me?" asked Carrie and nearly provoked a thunderstorm.

Miss White said, "He's got to come down some time, Mr Pickering. At least we know where he is while he's up there."

About five minutes later, Shane emerged from the gloom at the bottom of the staircase. He was out of breath and smelling suspiciously of cigarette smoke. Picasso looked like he was going to give him a clip round the ear but then thrust his hands in his pockets and strode away, not trusting himself to speak. Miss White followed him in the direction of the cathedral coffee shop.

"Do you think there's something going on between those two?" asked Carrie.

"Naw," said Shane, "she'd eat him for breakfast."

"We've only got half an hour," said Carrie, looking at Shane resentfully. I suggested we get postcards and guide books but Shane wanted to go and find the statue of Lady Godiva we'd seen from the coach.

"Well go on, peeping Tom," I said. Carrie looked torn.

"No; I'd rather stay with you," she said, linking my arm. Then disentangling herself for a moment, she thrust her hand in her bag and produced a parcel.

"Your birthday present."

We sat on the grass while I untied the tatty re-used ribbons. Inside was a beautiful long chiffon scarf with all my favourite blues and purples.

"You do like it?" she asked seriously.

"It's perfect," I answered simply and truthfully.

Awkwardly she got to her feet.

"I suppose since it's your birthday, we'd better make sure we get some postcards so your coursework is mega brilliant."

I went up to her and hugged her.

"Thanks; and, if you don't mind, I'd like to go back and look at the angels again."

Needless to say, we were one missing when it was time for the coach to leave. Shane arrived ten minutes late, clutching a McDonald's hamburger.

"Now we definitely won't have time to stop at the services," said the Art master triumphantly.

"Aw, sir!!" came the chorus.

* * *

"Party party party," sang Carrie skipping down the church hall with a bowl of sherry trifle.

"Is that girl right in the head?" asked Aunt Bev.

"They've been friends since they were little," said Mum apologetically.

"Yes, I remember," replied Aunt Bev. "Of course, Gerald and I sent our children to a private school."

Mum and I exchanged a secret smile. We were both enjoying ourselves and Aunt Bev's opinion of Carrie only added to the entertainment.

Mother was in her element.

"The maids of honour look beautiful," she commented with satisfaction.

"Maids of honour! That's not us, is it?" asked Carrie, appearing next to me.

"No, the almond cakes," I hissed and looked at the spread on the long trestle tables. Yes, the whole display was beautiful. In pride of place was a huge birthday cake with the iced words, "Sweet Sixteen". Mum had baked it herself.

"Time to put up the balloons," said Dad, pleased that he was being useful.

"I'm beginning to wonder who this party is for," I laughed.

"Well, it's a great achievement, getting you to sixteen," he said and I saw the truth of it. "You're not getting another at eighteen, you know. The next one will be when you get wed." He seemed to lose some of his enthusiasm.

"Sorry to lose your little girl?" I joked.

"No, just thinking that it will cost an arm and a leg," he said.

I watched him affectionately as he played with the balloons. Life wouldn't be the same if he didn't complain at the cost of everything.

Carrie went over to help him.

"It's extortionate the price of these things," he said, even though he hadn't paid for them.

"It's daylight robbery," Carrie agreed cheerfully. It was clear they liked each other and I was pleased. Yes, parties were fun, I decided.

Time flew as we put the finishing touches to the room and to the stage where the disc jockey would be. Aunt Bev had insisted on "someone professional, with experience," and we'd gone along with the idea but we'd still invited Greg to come to the party as a guest and to bring some of his mates. Carrie had taken the invitations and I'd grabbed the opportunity to send them a lyric inspired by the Coventry visit.

The disc jockey's helpers arrived to set up their lights and sound system just as we finished decorating the stage. They seemed to fancy themselves as "roadies" and carted the gear around with a lot of self-important huffing and puffing.

Carrie was sizing them up.

"Stop drooling," I said.

"They're too old," she sniffed. "Hope their music isn't ancient."

"Somebody recommended them when Aunt Bev booked the hall. They're used to this sort of do."

"That one just coming in; he's nice."

It was Bobby Cooke from the choir.

"Fancy that!" I exclaimed in surprise.

"Yes; I just said I did."

I gave her a friendly shove.

"What about these bigger fish you were going to fry?"

"Wait and see," she said. "I think this party might have some surprises for both of us."

"What do you mean?" I asked.

"Wait and see," she repeated.

"You'd better rush home and change, you two," said Mum. Carrie had left her clothes at our house. Her mum and brothers were coming to the party but her dad had sent his apologies because he was working away. At least, that's what Carrie's mum said. Carrie had seemed unwilling to talk about it and at this moment she didn't seem to care.

"My mum's lent me her best dress and it fits a treat," she said, bouncing towards the door and nearly colliding with Zeesham who was leading the way for his mother and his aunt who were carrying silver trays full of sweetmeats. They placed them on the tables. The two Asian women moved towards my mother each with their fingers placed together in a gesture of greeting and respect and they leaned gracefully towards her. Mother was totally taken aback. She didn't seem to know whether to curtsey or to bow. I hurried over and invited the whole family to the party.

* * *

The celebrations were in full swing. People were eating and chatting with the sound of pop tunes in the background. Greg and his friends hadn't arrived yet and Carrie occasionally glanced towards the door.

Dad and Uncle Arthur were supervising the table that served as a bar and Carrie's mum who sometimes worked as a barmaid was helping them. I'd been expecting a bit of a fuss when Aunt Bev discovered the church hall had a licence for alcohol but she merely said, "Splendid," and asked if we had any bowls for a fruit and wine punch. There were some cans of lager for the adults who wanted them and crates and crates of soft drinks.

"I think your Aunt Bev's quite crafty," said Carrie.

"How come?"

"Well, the booze is always a problem; unless you don't have any."

"My gran wouldn't like that," I said, smiling towards the corner where Gran was nursing her own little supply of Guinness.

"Think of some of the parties we've been to where things got out of hand."

66

"You've never complained before," I said, remembering Carrie being sick in a flowerpot.

"That wasn't OUR party!"

"I'm glad we didn't have it at home," I said as I looked across at Shane whom we'd invited after all. He was sitting with a large group from our school. Samantha and Paul were with them but they might as well have been on a different planet by themselves.

"I wonder if teachers often get invited to things like this," I said, looking across at Miss White. We'd both wanted her to come. She raised her glass towards us and smiled then turned her attention back to Zeesham's mum.

A crackling whistle issued from the microphone and we saw the disc jockey fiddling with it.

"It looks like he wants us to start dancing," said Carrie as another whistle pierced the chatter. Unconsciously she started swirling her skirt. She looked really pretty in the emerald green dress with a floaty patterned chiffon overskirt. It brought out the red glints in her hair. The dress was slightly too long for Carrie but that added to the charm. I wished my mum and I could share clothes. The thought made me smile. Not only was Mum twice my size but our tastes were completely different. The idea of her wearing my new blue taffeta was totally ridiculous.

"Do you think I should put a pin in the front of this?" asked Carrie.

"If you've got it, flaunt it!" I advised. She smiled gratefully and we turned our attention to the disc jockey. Earlier, he'd welcomed everybody, told a weak joke about his girlfriend being sixteen (sixteen stone) and introduced the medley of tunes he would play while we were eating.

"I hate his white shoes," I said, then noticed that Carrie was looking towards the door.

"Don't worry, they'll come," I said.

"Who?" she asked, "I was just looking for that roadie. The nice one."

"He's over there by the stage," I said and volunteered to introduce her.

"You're both looking very glamorous," said Bobby shyly as we approached.

I never knew what to say in reply to compliments. I couldn't very well answer, "What, this old thing?!" about my new blue taffeta.

"Thanks," said Carrie. "Aren't you going to introduce us properly, Sarah?"

She was so busy chatting up Bobby that she didn't notice Greg arriving, accompanied by half a dozen mates. Just at that moment, the disc jockey managed to conquer the microphone.

"Ladies and gentleman, take your partners for the military two-step."

Carrie and I looked at each other incredulously.

"The what?!"

"Don't worry," laughed Bobby. "It's a great ice-breaker. He'll shout the instructions, like at a barn dance. It'll help if you two start the dancing; and it's the proper thing to do, on an occasion like this."

Carrie promptly took his hand.

"You'd better help, then, hadn't you?"

"Greg's just arrived," I said. Carrie paused uncertainly but it was too late. Bobby was already leading her on to the floor. I hurried over to Dad and, though he pretended to be reluctant, he strutted quite proudly forward, encouraging everyone else to join in.

The circle of couples formed quickly. Uncle Arthur deserted his post to lead Carrie's mum into the dance. Carrie's two elder brothers took over dispensing the drinks. I had misgivings about that but saw Miss White rush over to give them a hand.

Bobby was right; it was great fun. Dad actually knew what to do and was surprisingly light on his feet. When everyone seemed to have got the hang of it, the dance was made progressive so that the inner circle, who were mostly male, moved forward to take a new partner.

Greg and his friends had joined in and I could see them gradually approaching. Carrie was in front of me and she kept turning to watch their progress too. Tim was the first to arrive and he told me the lyrics of my song were great. As Tim moved on to dance with Carrie, Greg took my hand. Carrie turned and smiled at us.

"Glad you could make it, Greg," she said.

"Long time no see, Sarah." Greg looked into my eyes, putting on the smile he knew worked the best. It left me cold but I managed a weak grin in return.

I sensed he didn't really care about me; it was just that he couldn't resist putting on the charm.

"Your lyrics are good," he said, "for a sixteen-year-old."

This time I smiled more naturally. Perhaps we could salvage something from that dustbin. I hoped it would be friendship. After all, we'd grown to know each other quite well.

"It's a quote, isn't it?" he asked. "In the song; the words, 'Live together or die like fools'."

"Yes. Martin Luther King. It's actually 'Live together like brothers or die together like fools', but I thought that sounded sexist."

"Thought it was him," Greg said.

"I hope we stay friends," I said.

"Yeah, why not?" he grinned and held me closer before he moved on to dance with Carrie.

"So you're the one who writes the songs," said my next partner, politely, taking my hand. They say a touch can be electric and it was true. I turned to look at him properly and saw a kind, honest face with a slightly hesitant expression and gentle grey-blue eyes. His dark hair was thick, smooth and short.

"I couldn't help overhearing," he said with embarrassment. "And I hope you don't mind me coming to the party."

"Mind?! Of course not!" I felt like shouting but I simply said he was welcome.

He moved on to dance with Carrie but the music stopped. A pop song was announced and we all stayed with our new partners apart from some of the adults who were flopping on chairs. I was dancing with another of Greg's mates whom I knew slightly. He was a good dancer but it was one of those numbers where you might as well be dancing by yourself. I saw Carrie chatting as she hopped about with more energy than grace and then I noticed Bobby watching her with obvious appreciation. Near him, Miss White was talking to Gran and I saw that each of them had a Guinness in her hand. Zeesham was next to us trying to teach an elderly relative in a sari to dance and I wondered what his angels would think of that. Samantha and Paul were making for the door, hand in hand. Miss White was watching them with an anxious frown but Gran was smiling sentimentally.

Next came the skaters' waltz and the compère decided it would be a progressive. I was praying the music wouldn't stop till I'd danced with the boy with the black hair and the nice eyes. He was getting nearer. One more partner and then . . .

"Hello again," he said.

I couldn't think how to get in all I wanted to say in the short time we would be dancing together and I ended up saying nothing.

"My name's Rick, short for Richard," he said eventually, "and I know you're Sarah." Then, "Do they ever shorten your name?" he went on when I didn't answer.

"No," I managed to reply and began to wonder why I hadn't got a nickname. The music stopped at that moment and we stood awkwardly, becoming conscious of our linked hands.

"Now for a waltz," shouted the compère.

"I can't waltz very well," said Rick, "but I can walk round to the music."

I laughed but words seemed to have failed me.

"We can walk round together," he said and added hesitantly, "if you like?"

"Oh I do like!" I managed to gasp.

He moved naturally to the music making it easy to follow him. I was dancing on clouds and very conscious of his closeness. All too soon, it was over. There was a short break and he led me to the drinks table. I was recovering my composure and starting to ask questions as we sat down.

"No, I haven't known Greg a long time," he replied, "I've only just been transferred here by the firm I work for." He passed some peanuts to me. "So you're sixteen today?"

"No, a week yesterday and Carrie's not sixteen till Monday."

"Well, happy birthday a week yesterday."

"Thanks."

"I'm eighteen. I left school to work in a bank."

I couldn't think how to get round to the question I really wanted to ask. You can't just blurt out, "Have you got a girlfriend?" He seemed tongue-tied too. He passed me the peanuts again.

"No thanks; I'll get too fat."

"You're just right as you are," he said, "and that blue suits you."

I blushed in reply to the compliment.

"I suppose your boyfriend tells you that too," he said awkwardly.

"I haven't got a boyfriend," I said, looking directly in his eyes and hoping I was giving the right signals to encourage him.

"What do you do in your spare time?" he asked.

I didn't know what to answer. If I said, "What spare time?" he'd think I was giving him the brush-off. If I said I spent my time writing songs and doing my homework, he'd think I was odd.

"At the moment I don't do very much," I said at last, "but there are lots of things I'd like to do."

"I know what you mean," Rick said. "I have to go on courses and study, so I don't get much time; but, when I do, there are things like going to see a film but I don't fancy going on my own."

"I like going to the pictures," I said. I didn't care if I sounded too eager.

"Look, I can't stay very long – in fact, I'm going to have to leave now . . . " Rick began, looking at his watch.

I felt my heart sink and I went crimson with embarrassment. What a fool I'd made of myself. I'd been too keen and I'd frightened him off. Then I realised he was still speaking.

"But I'd like to see you again," he said.

My heart leapt. It was like being on a see-saw or going up and down in a lift.

Now Rick was starting to look anxious.

"That's if you want to," he added.

And so we made a date for the next Tuesday.

"I'm sorry I have to rush off," he said. "I'm catching the late train to pop home for the rest of the weekend. It's my sister's birthday tomorrow."

He politely shook my hand as he was leaving and the formal gesture seemed very appealing. I noticed my mum looking on with approval. I felt like running up to her, flinging my arms around her, spinning her round and shouting, "I'm going to the pictures with him on Tuesday."

I couldn't believe how calmly I was standing there as I watched him push through the crowd of dancers to say goodbye to Greg and Carrie who were chatting earnestly at another table with Tim. I turned my attention to the rest of the guests and the whole world seemed a beautiful place. I even agreed to dance with Shane.

Soon afterwards, I saw Greg and Tim walk up to the stage. I noticed they'd got their guitars from the car. They had a word with the disc jockey and Greg took the microphone.

"Ladies and gentlemen. You all know it's Carrie's and Sarah's birthdays. Carrie has asked us as a special present to Sarah to let you hear our latest number. Sarah wrote the lyrics. We haven't worked out a full arrangement yet but here it is anyway."

It wasn't their usual style. They'd turned it into a sort of ballad where the pauses were as important as the music.

> "Injustice round you burning;
>   Red anger in the smoke;
> But rising from the ashes
>   A single wisp of hope.
> Ignore the chants of hatred
>   And sing this song of peace;
> One voice will join another,
>   The angels' song increase.
>   Live life together
>   Forgive each other
>   Or die together like fools.
>   Live life together
>   And help each other
>   For love is the golden rule."

*   *   *

At the end of the festivities, when Carrie and I had helped clear things away, we sank into a contented heap, leaning on each other.

"That was some party," said Carrie.

"I think Bobby fancies you," I said. "You'd better start coming to church. That's where I know him from."

She grinned and looked sideways at me.

"I'm glad Greg came."

"Yeah. I'm glad too," I said, thinking of the song. Mum and Dad had been so pleased.

"It's a pity his mate, Rick, had to go so soon," said Carrie. "We were so busy arranging about singing the song that we didn't get a chance to say goodbye to him properly."

73

"Yes," I said dreamily. "Guess what? I've got a date with him next Tuesday."

Carrie scrambled to her feet and stood with her hands on her hips.

"I hope you're pleased with yourself," she said.

"What's that supposed to mean? What ARE you talking about?"

"After all I've done for you!"

"Done for me?"

"I got Greg to come here. Tim and I planned it."

"What?"

"We planned it so you could get back together with Greg. You used to tell me how different he was. I knew that's what you wanted."

"I didn't! I don't!"

"No! You don't NOW all right!"

Realisation dawned as she said bitterly, "You got off with the bloke I fancied; I invited him to the party for ME!"

*   *   *

It was Monday registration.

"It's Carrie's birthday today, miss," said Sam.

"Yes, I hadn't forgotten. Thankyou, Samantha. Besides which, I would have known it had to be something unusual because Carrie's not talking for once."

"I'm just not talking to HER," announced Carrie, now she was sure she had the attention of the whole class.

Very deliberately, she took her chair with her and moved to another table. Before she sat down, she huffed, "The stunts Some People will play on your birthday!"

3

"Rick works in a bank," I said and Dad made a little noise which I took as a sign of approval, though he continued reading his paper.

"He looked very respectable," Mum said. "How old is he?"

"Eighteen," I replied. Conversations were so much easier when you were telling the truth. Certainly they were less effort on your memory, I decided.

"Did you hear that?" Mum asked Aunt Bev who was peering at a railway timetable. "He works in a bank."

Aunt Bev looked up and smiled. I half expected her to remind us about the good job her son had in Australia and her son-in-law in Canada but she merely said, "He seemed a very pleasant young man when he came to call for you, Sarah."

I'd already told them about the film we'd seen and I wanted to go into all the details of the evening but some things are impossible to share. I lapsed into silence, nursing my cup of coffee and my memories of the moment at the door when he'd kissed me good night.

As we washed up afterwards, Mum said, "So you had a good evening?"

"Terrific."

"He brought you back at a sensible time. You should have invited him in for some coffee. We wouldn't have minded, you know."

"I know," I said and added hastily, "he had to get up early for work." I hadn't wanted to invite him in because I was afraid it would be an anticlimax to a perfect evening.

75

"Let's sit down and you can tell me all about it."

I sat down but I didn't know where to start.

"You seemed very nervous when you were getting ready," she prompted. "You looked a treat though."

"Thanks. You're right, I was nervous. I thought he might have forgotten or lost the paper I wrote the address on; or changed his mind." There were other reasons too. I had been nervous about the way they would behave when he arrived. I'd dreaded Mum fussing or Dad showing me up by going on about not staying out late. But I couldn't tell her that. In fact, they had been very pleasant though I had sensed them looking him up and down for clues about the sort of boy he was. He must have passed the test. Another reason I was nervous was that I dreaded him being a disappointment when I saw him again and that he wouldn't match the boy I had been day dreaming about. But he had been everything I hoped for and so was the evening.

Mum seemed to be wanting to ask another question but was having difficulty selecting the words. What was it she wanted to know, I wondered. Did she long to ask if we'd sat in the back row?

"Of course cinemas were very different when I was young. Our local one was called the Palace and that's what it seemed like to me, a palace – though I called it the flea-pit just like everybody else did. It's been pulled down now, of course." She smiled sadly yet fondly at the memory. Surely, she didn't used to sit in the back row?

"It was just a small studio," I explained, " . . . and we sat in the middle." That was true; the back seats were already taken and I think Rick was relieved. He obviously didn't want to move too fast and for the first time I thought about the problems boys face when they go on a date. The film was nearly over before he plucked up courage to hold my hand. I sensed him thinking about it for ages so eventually I decided that when there was a suitable moment in the film I would grip his arm. He understood the signal and took my hand. His touch was just as electric as when we danced at my birthday party. I squeezed his palm and relaxed into the pleasure of being with him.

"He's not a bit like Greg," I said. "He's shy and polite."

It was the first time I'd spoken honestly and truthfully to Mum about Greg.

"That was the young man who sang your song, wasn't it? He did it very well. Dad and I felt very proud."

"Did Dad recognise who he was?"

"No; I don't think so . . . and I thought I would leave him with the idea of the brass band," she smiled.

I looked at her curiously. I had imagined that it would be difficult to talk to her about Greg because I'd told so many lies. Was it possible that she hadn't been taken in? Had she been reading between the lines all the time?

"You forget," she went on, "I was your age once. You think I don't remember what it was like to be young. I once told my own mum that your dad was a wonderful conversationalist. She's never let me forget it." She smiled and added, "It's nice being able to talk together."

My mind was in a turmoil. Here we were, talking at last, and I felt I was meeting a stranger. She wasn't like my mum at all and I wasn't sure how I felt about it.

"You're very like I was at your age." I greeted that information with barely suppressed horror and felt very guilty at my reaction. "Would I grow up like her?" I thought, as Mum continued.

"Carrie's like her mum, isn't she? I thought Mrs Johnson was looking very pretty. She's kept her figure, hasn't she?"

By now I had nothing to say at all.

"I'm beginning to think Carrie's turning into a nice young woman," Mum went on, managing not to add, "after all" and seeming not to notice that I wasn't replying.

"And wasn't it nice of her to ask them to sing your song? Is she pleased about your new boyfriend?"

So there was something about Rick I had to tell lies about, after all.

"Yes," I replied, through clenched teeth.

*　　*　　*

Carrie was definitely not pleased. She milked the situation for all it was worth and you would have thought she'd been engaged to Rick, the way she went on about it.

Samantha had taken Carrie's side and around school I found them arm in arm with Sam giving me cold glances as she consoled Carrie. Sam's boyfriend, Paul, tagged along behind them hoping for a return to normality. Shane had been stirring the quarrel but when I didn't rise to the bait, he left me alone. Zeesham was the only one who ignored the conflict and behaved in his usual friendly manner.

Miss White had observed the situation without comment but she decided our tutor room needed some new displays and I was given the task.

"You've really been sent to Coventry," she laughed one lunchtime. "Don't worry; it will blow over," she said cheerfully and she was right.

It was as if Carrie set time limits on her various grudges. Before the end of the week, she was back sitting next to me and the rest of the class took their lead from her.

"I haven't finished my Maths homework," she said.

I was tempted to ignore her but instead I smiled and reached in my bag for my exercise book.

"Glad to have you back," I said.

"Let's forget it," she muttered.

It was lunchtime before she asked about Rick. I knew we'd have to talk about it some time; we couldn't go on avoiding mentioning him; and I felt relieved when she brought the matter up.

"Well, how did the date go on Tuesday?" she asked.

"I haven't seen him since then; he's gone on a course for a day or two. He's rung me."

"That's more than Greg used to do," she said.

"Yeah," I admitted ruefully.

"Is it the real thing?"

"Dunno." I didn't feel I could confide in her yet.

"Are you going to church again?"

"Yes," I replied. "We were too tired last Sunday after the party but we'll go this week. Aunt Bev is going home on Monday morning so it's her last Sunday. We'll be visiting Gran in the nursing home in the morning so I expect we'll go to the evening service."

"Can I come?" asked Carrie to my surprise. "I think we both ought to go," she went on. "After all, we did use their hall for the party."

I wasn't used to Carrie feeling a sense of obligation. Perhaps my mum was right about the change in her. Then I remembered her interest in Bobby Cooke who sang in the choir. It also crossed my mind that maybe Bobby was the reason she had started talking to me again.

*   *   *

"There's a letter for you, Sarah," said Mum on Saturday morning. Aunt Bev had gone to book her ticket and Dad was already working his way through the post, frowning at the bills.

As she handed the envelope to me, Mum commented, "There's no stamp on it. Must have been delivered by hand."

At first I thought it was a late birthday card and moved away in case it was one of those "sixteen is sexteen" cards I wouldn't want my parents to see. But it was too flimsy to be a card. Maybe it was a thankyou letter about the party.

As soon as I read, "Sarah, my love," I turned to the back page but it only said, "Your ardent admirer." I rushed up to my room to read it in private.

"From the moment our eyes met and you smiled, I knew that we were meant for each other."

I flopped on the bed and carried on reading.

"You are like the rose that blooms in the desert, wasting its sweetness on the desert air." I felt like dancing round the room. What a wonderful love letter!

"Always wear blue," it said. "I knew it was your colour, mirrored in your eyes; deep as the timeless ocean, brilliant as the azure skies; eternal, spiritual and pure. I will love you for ever; your eyes, your soul and your mind."

"Wow! Wow! Wow!" I screeched and ran round the room in ecstasy. He was everything I had ever hoped for and I couldn't wait until our next meeting.

The phone call on the previous Thursday night had been a bit of a disappointment and he had apologised for being inarticulate on the phone. He was using a pay booth and ran out of change. His last words had been, "I'll be back by the weekend but I've got to write up a report. See you Tuesday; same time . . ."

I ran down the stairs; I couldn't show Mum the letter but I thought I'd tell her about it. I knew she must have heard me whooping and I was surprised she hadn't already shouted up to see if I was all right. But there was deathly silence in the lounge. Dad was holding an official looking letter and staring into space. Mum was clutching his arm as if to give support. She turned her head towards me and said quietly, "The warehouse is closing down. Your father's been made redundant."

*   *   *

I'd invited Carrie for the whole of Sunday but the atmosphere in our house was so depressing I wondered if I ought to cancel the arrangement.

"No," said Mum, who seemed to be taking Dad's news in her stride, "life must go on as normally as possible. Isn't that right, Dad?"

She didn't expect an answer and received none. He had been slumped in his chair most of Saturday, staring at the sport on TV and seeing nothing. He had only gone to the pub because Mum and Aunt Bev insisted that they needed to find out what was going on in the outside world.

I was glad really that Carrie was spending Sunday with us. I had wanted to make sure that the quarrel was definitely over when I first invited her but now there were other reasons. Carrie had problems of her own, as I had discovered on Friday night in the café when we had been planning the Sunday. Bobby Cooke was no longer significant; she was simply desperate to get out of their flat.

"Dad's even taken the goldfish," she said. "He won it somewhere. I hope it dies. I hope he wakes up one morning and finds it floating at the top of the bowl." She pulled a face that was meant to resemble a dead goldfish. "I'm working all day Saturday at that shoe shop I told you about," she went on, "and I'll be glad to come over to you for the day on Sunday."

"What about your mum? Shouldn't you be spending some time helping her get over it?"

"There's a bloke doing that," she said bleakly. "I hope he doesn't last long. He's all right, I suppose, and I'm making quite a bit of money from him 'to go to the pictures' or wherever. I'll get quite a packet for being out all Sunday. I'll tell him I'm going to an amusement park."

*　　*　　*

When we arrived at the nursing home, Gran was pleased to see us and surprised everybody by recognising Carrie and remembering the party.

"I had a friend," she said. "Lizzie. She buried three husbands. But she's gone too, now. We had birthdays near together and we went to a barn dance. I wore a blue gingham dress. Lizzie had one the same, only it was pink. We danced every dance, you know. Lizzie's brother was one of my admirers. He was very handsome but his eyes were too close together. Never trust people whose eyes are too close together." Gran stopped

81

talking to adjust her false teeth which seemed to be slipping and then looked round at each of us in turn. Her eyes fastened on Aunt Bev.

"Where's little Evelyn and those young imps, Richard and Malcolm? Are they away at school? You shouldn't have let Gerald talk you into sending them away."

"Hush, Mother," said Aunt Bev. "The firm was paying for their private education and that was long ago. Look, we've brought some Guinness for you."

"It does you good," said Gran gleefully.

After a while, Carrie and I went for a walk in the grounds. I was wanting to tell her about the love letter but I felt awkward about mentioning Rick.

"I wonder if your gran's right about eyes," she said. "No offence meant but that's the only thing wrong with your Rick." Immediately I bridled thinking it was sour grapes on her part but I managed not to comment. We walked along in silence and then I decided that we ought to iron out the matter of Rick once and for all.

"Look, I'm sorry about what happened with Rick. I honestly had no idea that you fancied him."

"I know," she said, linking my arm, "but don't let's talk about that."

I agreed but in view of what happened later, I wish we had.

*   *   *

Aunt Bev had packed her belongings ready for leaving the next day. Carrie and I thanked her for the party.

"Well, you two. Sixteen is a good age. I wish I could remember my sixteenth birthday clearly. Until your party I hadn't realised how time makes one's memory selective. It's as if I can't recall the actual events; I can only remember talking about them. I'm going to look at my album when I get home. Maybe it will jog my memory. I know I have a photo of me as Delilah and I hope I can find out who played Samson."

"Perhaps you'll remember all the details when you get older, like Sarah's gran," said Carrie.

"Yes. My mother certainly seems to remember everything," agreed Aunt Bev but there was something odd in her tone.

"Mum and Dad will miss you too," I said politely, sensing she wanted to change the subject.

"Possibly," she replied and once again I found I was looking in on an adult world which I didn't understand fully.

Carrie's misfortunes seemed to be making her more sensitive to other people. She commented sympathetically, "It must be awful to have your children so far away. Australia. Canada."

"They are always near me in my thoughts," said Aunt Bev, "however far away they are," and I knew she was including Richard. You can't be farther away than dead.

"Well, you two," Aunt Bev said again, "enjoy being sixteen. I wish that I had understood that you are only one age for one year."

"What a funny thing to say," commented Carrie to me soon afterwards.

"It's true, though, isn't it?" I answered. "You are, say, fourteen; you are fifteen; you are sixteen and so on. How did you spend that year?"

"That's deep!" laughed Carrie.

"No, honestly," I said. "We ought to be doing some serious thinking about the future. We need to plan it properly. It's not like making up your mind what we're going to do at the weekend."

Suddenly I realised I sounded like my mum. She was always going on about "the future".

"Take each day as it comes," advised Carrie.

* * *

Evening Service was fairly predictable except that Bobby Cooke sang a solo. His voice had developed into a pleasant tenor and listening to him took me back in time to the years when I'd fancied him. But that was definitely in the past. I sneaked a glance at Carrie and it confirmed what I had suspected. There was a predatory glint in her eye.

Afterwards coffee and biscuits were served in the church hall. Carrie was looking round and as if on cue, Bobby came up to us. With him was his friend, another member of the choir called Branwell.

I recognised him from my Sunday school days. He always beat me getting gold stars. I couldn't remember what the stars were for but I did remember that he was very earnest and conscientious about everything. When the rest of the group were acting the fool, he and I had been the boring, perfect pupils.

"That's a funny name," said Carrie, studying the stocky, dark-haired young man who blinked at us seriously from behind his thick-rimmed glasses.

"The brother of the Brontë sisters was called Branwell," I said and commented that I thought it was a lovely name.

"I expected that you would recognise it," he said.

"And I recognise you too," I smiled. "You were in my class in Sunday school."

"I run that class now," he said, "though I might have to give it up for a while because of the pressure of exams."

He explained he was in the sixth form at a neighbouring boys' school.

"What do you want to stay on at school for?" said Carrie. "I can't wait to leave."

I knew she felt like that but it still came as a jolt. I wanted to stay on but I couldn't imagine school without Carrie.

"I wish I was still at school," said Bobby. "They're the best days of your life, so they say."

"What a depressing thought!" Carrie laughed. "If they're the best, I don't want to know about the rest!"

"I've always thought that was a stupid statement," I commented. "If school leaves you thinking that was the

84

best time of your life, then they haven't prepared you for growing up."

"That's very perceptive, Sarah," said Branwell.

"I still wish I could have stayed on though," said Bobby. "I'm working in an insurance office but I'm taking exams at night school."

I smiled at him sympathetically. I knew his mother was a widow and guessed that money was tight at home. I looked to where my parents were chatting with Aunt Bev and I realised how lucky I was. Both of them were keen for me to stay on at school though I suspected it was because they thought I'd have better prospects in the marriage market. A sudden thought hit me. "What about Dad's redundancy? Would that change things?"

"Watch your cup, Sarah," said Carrie but it was too late. I'd relaxed my hold slightly and a thin dribble of coffee dripped from my saucer down the lapel of my jacket. Carrie held my cup while I fished in my pocket for a paper hanky. Branwell was already proffering one.

"Thanks," I said dabbing at the stain. "It's all right, I don't think it will show."

"Hope not," said Bobby. "That's a nice jacket."

"What, this old thing?"

"You look good in blue."

I suppressed a smile, thinking of Rick's letter. It was great to have a second opinion.

"Well, it's my favourite colour," I said lightly, knowing that Carrie was getting fed up with the compliments about my jacket.

"Blue is a spiritual colour," added Branwell earnestly. Carrie stared at him and wrinkled her nose. She had never met anybody as serious as Branwell and she was having trouble placing him in any category. It was mutual. He too seemed to be having difficulty accommodating her in his world view.

"You going to be a vicar?" asked Carrie bluntly. I suspected it was meant to be a put-down but Branwell took it at face value.

"One has to have a vocation to train for the ministry," he replied solemnly, peering at her over the top of his spectacles.

"Have you had the call?" I asked quickly, sensing that Carrie was going to ask what holidays had got to do with it. I managed to put the question in a friendly tone and with a fairly straight face.

Branwell launched into a slightly pompous speech about the difference between one's aspirations and true inspiration. I caught Bobby's eye. He was clearly enjoying this encounter between Branwell and Carrie. I found myself giving him a wink. He grinned and hastily passed round a plate of biscuits.

"Do you mean you really want to be a vicar?" asked Carrie incredulously. She blinked and looked across at our vicar who was embarrassing my parents by saying how pleased he was that they had come back to the fold while Aunt Bev looked on with her hands clasped across her chest as if she felt she had fulfilled her duty to her youngest brother.

Branwell informed us that until he felt the divine call he was content to train as a chartered accountant though he felt that "the spiritual dimension of life was of vast importance and he was aware of the dichotomy between religious values and those of his chosen area of study."

"He's a real weirdo," said Carrie to me later. "You need a dictionary to talk to him."

The vicar was doing his rounds. We were next on the list.

"I see you know Bob and Branwell. We're having a sponsored walk next Saturday afternoon; perhaps you'd like to come."

"I warn you, it's rain gear and wellies at this time of year," grimaced Bobby. "I'm the leader."

Carrie promptly agreed that we would join in.

"What about your Saturday job?" I asked as the vicar turned to talk to a departing parishioner and Branwell told Bobby that he was going on the walk too.

"Anybody can be sick for a day," Carrie answered impatiently. There was a lull in our conversation. Bobby looked round the room for inspiration and must have remembered the party.

"I liked the song you wrote, Sarah."

"I arranged for them to play that," Carrie chipped in, "and that was a good song you sang in church."

Bobby went pink and simply said, "Thanks."

"I was surprised to see that you were in the choir last time I was here," I said to help the conversation along. "I thought you'd given up singing."

"So did I when my voice broke a few years back," he admitted ruefully. "It made me think a lot about changes and learning to live with them."

"You're getting as bad as him," groaned Carrie and Branwell took this as a cue to ask what my song was about.

"Forgiveness," I said as Carrie grimaced.

"Forgive and forget, I always say," she laughed. I smiled because in my experience she rarely did either.

"It isn't as easy as that," retorted Branwell.

The vicar was back with us. "Yes, Branwell, but Jesus said we must forgive seventy times seven offences."

"How many times is that?" asked Carrie, trying to work it out in her head.

"Four hundred and ninety," said Branwell instantly.

"What about the four hundred and ninety-first?" asked Carrie.

The vicar smiled. "It's a way of saying every time. We must be careful not to take the Bible too literally."

I found his smug smirk irritating.

"Jesus Himself is our example," he said serenely. "Even when He was dying he said, 'Father forgive them; they know not what they do.'" He clasped his hands over his paunch and prepared to move on.

"But what if they do know what they're doing?" asked Carrie. The vicar pretended not to hear and moved away.

"Well even then," Branwell said, "you're supposed to love your enemies."

"You've to love them; you don't have to like them," I added with a smile, trying to lighten the conversation.

"I suppose the important thing is not to hate them," agreed Bobby.

"I don't know about the enemies; I find it hard to love my friends sometimes," Carrie laughed, grinning at me.

I grinned back but I knew I would think about these ideas later.

My parents came over before the vicar had a chance to get round to them again. Branwell and Bobby said they would walk along with us.

"It's quite a long way," I said.

"We know," said Bobby, "but we're enjoying your company."

We chatted mostly about the sponsored walk and Carrie was very enthusiastic.

"I like playing Follow My Leader," she said, batting her eyelashes for all she was worth.

Bobby didn't seem to be responding to the signals. As we said our goodbyes, he murmured to me, "I was talking to her at the party. It seems strange to me that you two are such good friends."

I felt a sinking feeling. We were going to need those wellies.

*   *   *

Carrie brought her coursework round on Monday evening so we could work together.

"You know I've got a date with Rick tomorrow night, don't you?" I asked pointedly, remembering how irritated Greg used to be when Carrie tagged along.

"It's all right, I'm going out with Nita tomorrow."

"Nita?"

It turned out Nita worked at the shoe shop and was about eighteen.

"She's engaged to a chiropodist," said Carrie as if that was a great achievement.

"They must have a lot in common," I joked.

"Feet," I explained when she didn't laugh.

Obviously, in Carrie's eyes, Nita was not to be taken lightly but to be seen as a source of inspiration.

"Sorry; it was a corny gag," I giggled but she didn't smile. I couldn't resist adding, "Looks like I've put my foot in it."

"I can't smell anything," she said and slowly started to grin. "The old jokes are still the best," she added, "but you'd better stop it or I'll put the boot in!" We both cracked up in a fit of laughter.

"Seriously," Carrie said, "you'll like Nita. She says there might be a proper job going for me when she leaves to get married. He works in London so she'll be moving."

"Perhaps you'd better work on Saturday instead of going on the walk. It won't look good if you skive off," I advised.

"No, it's all right. Honest. It's all arranged. I'm working late night opening on Thursday and Friday instead."

We carried on writing up our coursework and then suddenly she asked, "What are you going to wear on your feet? On Saturday."

"Cut off wellies," I said, remembering my premonitions about the walk.

"Nita's given me a pair of black suede boots. They're quite smart but they need to stretch a bit. I've stuffed damp newspaper in them."

"Why don't you wear your trainers? You'll need to be comfortable."

"You sound more like your mother every day," she said, peering over at my coursework.

"It's supposed to be your own work," I grumbled.

"I was only checking. And, anyway, Samantha's dad does all her coursework. That's why he was so cross when she got a low grade last time."

We worked in silence until Mum brought in some ham sandwiches with the edges daintily cut off and steaming mugs of coffee.

"I wish my mum was more like yours," said Carrie munching happily.

"Are you going to the shed this week?" I asked.

"Yes. I'm taking Nita. She was really impressed when I said I knew Monolith. She thinks their music is great."

I suppressed a giggle at the thought of Greg's new groupie being a chiropodist's girlfriend.

"Will you take my new song?" I asked, going to my bag to find the words. Carrie looked at the lyric. "'The Biggest of All Mod Cons'," she read. "What on earth are you writing about now?"

"Modern conveniences," I explained. "You know, fridges and freezers."

"I thought conveniences were lavatories," she said. I groaned and she carried on reading out loud.

> "She's got a fridge and freezer
> To make life easier
> > With her newly wedded
> > And bedded
> > Love.
> > With the very biggest
> > The best and biggest
> > Of all mod cons.
>
> "She's in the housewife coven
> Magic in the oven
> > Pushing round the hoover
> > To prove her
> > Love.
> > With the very biggest
> > The best and biggest
> > Of all mod cons.
>
> "Pots and pans she'll clean for sure
> Carpets and furniture

Curtains and the rest in
Her nest of
Love.
With the very biggest
The best and biggest
Of all mod cons.

"Youth and joy are flying past
Aches and pains growing fast
            Cleaning out the knife stand
            She dreams of
            Love
            With the very biggest
            The best and biggest
            Of all mod cons.

"A disillusioned matron
In a frilly apron
            Polishing the silver
            To kill her
            Love.
            For Love was the biggest
            Love was the biggest
            Of all mod cons."

Carrie finished reading and sat back with a puzzled frown.

"It's a bit sexist," she said.

"That's the point," I muttered.

"Is it about your mother?" she asked. "Does she want to kill your dad? I know mine does."

"No," I said hastily. "It's about the way the media and the magazines sell the dream of married bliss." I nearly added, "And the books you read," but I simply said, "And the advertisers play on the same idea."

Even as I was talking I knew that the words had been about my mother when I started writing but now they could be about me. I was dreaming of Rick and myself. In the fantasy I was taking on the role of housewife. I wouldn't see it as slavery in the kitchen. I'd willingly give up my freedom, gladly wash and iron his shirts, cook his meals, fetch and carry. Just like my mother. All the things I'd decided I didn't want to do for Greg, I would revel in.

"But what I felt for Greg was just infatuation," I thought to myself. "That fleeting passion wasn't real love. Real love is . . . " But there the thought ended. I was beginning to understand what love wasn't; but I had no words to describe what it was.

*   *   *

As Carrie was about to leave, Dad announced to the furniture and anyone who was listening that he'd just pop down the road a minute. "To see what's happening in the world," Mum mouthed and smiled naughtily. She asked him to see Carrie on to the bus.

After they left, she said contentedly, "He's coming to terms with it." I followed her into the kitchen knowing that this was a new chapter in all our lives.

"Don't you ever feel trapped?" I asked.

"Not as much as he did. Going out every day to that warehouse. The sad thing is that he stayed there and worked his way up to supervisor because he thought there was security in it. He was thinking of us."

"How are we going to manage?" I asked.

"I don't know," she said. "The redundancy money will pay off the mortgage and then we'll have to see. I could go out to work perhaps. I used to work in the Post Office. I liked that . . . " She sighed. "Well, I suppose I'll be able to get a job as a cleaner somewhere."

"What about me?" I asked, biting my lip. "Perhaps I should start applying for jobs."

"You'll do no such thing." The tone was harsh but the motive was genuine. I thought of the sacrifices she had made in her life, big and little, for the people she loved. That was the moment I realised that love covered such a large range of feelings and actions. "Love" was a totally inadequate word because it had to be interpreted to fit the situation whenever you used it. Perhaps I would put the word in the dustbin.

* * *

Tuesday had arrived at last. I was counting the days; then the hours; then finally the minutes. Spot on time, Rick was at the door. Dad had slumped into a depression again and though Mum assured me it was temporary, I grabbed my jacket and rushed Rick out through the door.

"You're not embarrassed when I pick you up at your house?" he asked.

"No, it's just that things are difficult at home at present."

"What's wrong?"

"Dad's been made redundant," I said, happy that I could share my worries.

"Redundant with a golden handshake?" Rick asked.

"It'll pay off the mortgage but Mum reckons things will be difficult."

Rick didn't reply and we walked hand in hand to the cinema. He was very quiet.

"You've not much to say for yourself," I laughed, squeezing his hand and noticing rough calluses on his palm.

"I've been painting some woodwork in my digs," he explained. "The landlady is old and I thought I'd help to do the place up."

I was pleased to think he was practical as well as poetic.

"We'll have to get here earlier next week," I said. "The back seats have gone again."

I expected him to understand the joke but he seemed preoccupied. We sat in the middle of the studio and though we continued to hold hands, he didn't make any other romantic move. In some ways, I was glad because the film was engrossing and I was looking forward to comparing ideas afterwards. It seemed like bliss to me; holding hands, sharing popcorn and wallowing in the same sentiments while the screen enveloped us in its make-believe world.

He had little to say about the movie as we walked home afterwards but the magic of the cinema always left me feeling unreal so I was happy just walking and dreaming in the frosty night, conscious of his closeness and our intertwining fingers. There was some vague chatter about the events of the previous week but we were back outside our house before I remembered to mention the letter.

"Well, my ardent admirer, when am I going to see you again? Your rose has been wilting in the desert air."

"What?" he asked, looking genuinely puzzled.

"The rose that blooms in the desert air," I prompted but already the truth was dawning on me.

"You did send me a letter?" I demanded.

"Letter," he said, "I'm worse at letter writing than I am on the phone."

*　　*　　*

I didn't invite him in, even though I knew Mum had baked some cakes specially. I felt humiliated and kept remembering those last comments I'd made which would sound so dreadfully over the top without the context of the letter. I leaned against the door. He hadn't kissed me good night; in fact he'd seemed anxious to get away; and we hadn't arranged to meet again.

"What did I do wrong?" I demanded of my mum when she came towards me, drying her hands on her apron.

We sat in the kitchen in the scent of newly baked buns and I wept.

"No boy is worth crying over," said Mum. "You have to keep your self-respect."

"But I don't know what I did," I blubbered.

"Now, now," consoled Mum with her arm around my shoulders, "Have a nice cup of hot chocolate and try to get some sleep."

*   *   *

I lay on my bed and when my tears had exhausted themselves I looked at the letter. Rick didn't write it; so who did? Was there another fish in the sea Carrie was always talking about? Then an awful thought struck me. Was the letter an elaborate hoax by Carrie? Was she getting her revenge or simply having a bit of fun at my expense? But who could she have persuaded to write it? Nobody that we knew had such beautiful handwriting. I fell into a dream of doubt and despair and woke up exhausted.

*   *   *

"What's up with you?" asked Carrie next morning.

"Nothing," I said abruptly.

"Who you kidding? Pull yourself together. You look like death warmed up. Come on. Get a grip, girl."

It was break before I had a chance to tell her that the great romance was over. Old habits die hard and in the cold light of day I had decided that the letter was not worth bothering about and I had to talk to Carrie. She listened as I recounted the events of the previous evening.

"What do expect with a guy like that?" she asked.

"What do you mean?"

"Well it was obvious he had an eye for the main chance."

"Talk English," I said.

"When we were dancing at the party, he said to me that the do must have cost an arm and a leg. As soon as I told him that your family paid for it, not mine, he didn't want to know me."

"Why didn't you tell me?"

"You didn't want to listen; and, anyway, I thought I might be wrong. And there was another thing. I felt I was to blame for you and Greg splitting up, one way and another. I didn't want to do that again."

Suddenly I realised that Carrie knew much more about people and their relationships than I did.

"Rick's a con artist," she said. "Maybe it takes one to know one. You've just got to face it. You've got to learn from it." Now she was beginning to sound like my mum.

"You say he seemed to lose interest when you told him your dad was made redundant," she went on. "You've got to think yourself into his shoes. There he is, working on the roofs and doing a bit of selling when the weather's bad . . ."

"What?" I interrupted but I knew she was telling the truth. She didn't go on. She knew I had been spun a line and she didn't want to be the one to make me admit it.

I knew she had hit the nail on the head. Rick was a liar. He couldn't help himself any more than I could in the past when the web of deceit spun its subtle thread. I had not only fallen for his lies but I had innocently passed on the deception when I had talked honestly, as I thought, to my parents. "What is love?" had been my preoccupation recently. Now I saw it was caught up with another question: "What is truth?" I didn't know which was the more complicated.

*   *   *

I sleepwalked through the day and thankfully staggered through our front door. There was an envelope on the mat.

My darling Sarah,
    Words fail me but I have to put pen to paper. I worship you, my blue angel. I think of nothing else but you. When I saw you again I loved you instantly. When

you spoke, I knew I had no words. When you laughed,
I wanted to weep. You speak to my soul and I dare not
reply. Except to breathe, I love you.

It was signed again by my anonymous ardent admirer.

I held the paper at arm's length. I knew it was not from Rick. Of that, I was sure. I didn't whoop round the room in ecstasy. I sat silently looking at it. I was still in shock from the demolition of my dreams about Rick and myself so I felt numb. I wondered how I would have felt if there had not been the misunderstanding about Rick's authorship. How would I have received these letters if they had come out of the blue? They held beautiful sentiments but unless I knew who wrote them they had no meaning for me. The right words about love and yet they inspired . . . what? The only feeling I recognised in the jumble of my emotions was . . . fear.

*　　*　　*

Thursday. Another letter.

"My dearest darling blue angel love, Keep yourself for me alone . . . "

The words were those you would want to read in a love letter but now they were corrupting all the vocabulary that once had meaning for me. I decided that I would get up early the next morning and lie in wait to see who delivered the unstamped letters.

But when I got home that afternoon there was another one on the mat. "You are the light of my life; the sunshine in my soul . . . " Could Carrie really have found someone to write in this way? Did she really hate me so much? I knew the thought was stupid but it persisted.

I remembered the first letter. "When first you smiled." "Wearing blue." It must be someone who was at the birthday party when I wore my electric blue dress.

"OK," I thought to myself, "why can't I accept that somebody fancies me and likes me to wear blue?"

Why couldn't I accept the letters without this feeling of persecution?

"Somebody who saw me at the dance," I thought. Bobby crossed my mind but I knew his handwriting; it couldn't have changed so much in recent years. I worked my way through all the members of our class who had been at the birthday celebrations. Shane was Carrie's friend. No way. Shane could barely spell his own name. Zeesham. He was the most literate boy in our class and the style was like his strange usage of English. If he was in on this strange plot I would feel suicidal, I decided. He was one of the few people I always felt at ease with. I knew he felt the same and if he had betrayed our relationship I would have caved in.

I was so certain that he was nothing to do with it that I confided in him.

"Zeesham," I said, "I've been getting these strange love letters."

He listened to me seriously and then he said, "You must ask your angels but I think these are not letters of love. They are letters of the germs in the soul." He thought for a while then added, "I think this person loves himself, not you."

*　　*　　*

"Sticks and stones may break my bones," I kept saying to myself, "but words will never hurt me." But they did.

Friday's letter had come by post and it was full of praise for my unique understanding of love in action. The quotations obscured the sense. It ended as usual, "Your ardent admirer." It contaminated everything I held dear; my favourite quotations and the sentiments I had hoped one day would come from the lips of my destined lover. The "ardent admirer" had squashed a winter rose at the end of the page and fixed it in place with Sellotape. I felt sad for the rose and sorry for myself.

*　　*　　*

By Saturday I had lost interest in life but Carrie was full of it.

"Come on," she said, "you can't carry on moping for ever. We've got to get fit for the walk."

"We can't get fit in one morning," I protested. "What do you intend doing? Going jogging?"

"I've got lots of loot," she grinned, "I'll treat you to a swim and a sauna."

"Sauna! We've never been to a sauna!"

"There's a first time for everything and Nita says the steam will help stretch my boots."

So there we were, emerging from the changing cubicles with towels wrapped round our swimming costumes and Carrie wearing her boots.

"Are you sure you know what you're doing?" I asked.

"Of course. Can you work out what to do with these lockers?"

"You put in fifty pence and you get it back later," said a middle-aged woman emerging from behind a curtain.

"What's in there, behind the curtain?" asked Carrie.

"It's a solarium. I'm trying to get a tan started before I go off for a winter holiday in the sun. Is this your first time here?"

I said yes and Carrie said no. When I frowned, Carrie admitted the truth rather grudgingly.

The lady pointed out the door of the sauna and warned us not to spend more than fifteen minutes in there at a time. She looked dubiously at Carrie's boots.

"I'm stretching them."

The lady burst out laughing, told us her name was Francine and waited while we put our belongings in the lockers. She escorted us to the door of the sauna and we went in.

It took a moment to get accustomed to the gloom and we paused with the door open.

"Close the door please," said a voice. We apologised and scrambled on to the nearest vacant wooden bench. Gradually I began to make out our surroundings and the people. There were three layers of benches on two sides of the small room and glowing coals in a fenced-off area in a corner.

"It's hottest at the top," said Francine. There was nobody sitting on the top layer. Two young women in scanty bikinis were lying out flat on the middle row and we three were sitting upright on the lowest seats. Adjacent to us was a middle-aged Asian gentleman wrapped in a huge towel.

He walked over to a wooden bucket. Grasping the handle of a ladle he sprinkled water on the coals. A hissing cloud of steam billowed round us. One of the girls sat up with a splutter.

"Wow," she said, "I think I've had enough."

"Me too," said the other and they both scrambled down from the benches. As they left, a man was entering. We could see a six-foot silhouette but it took a moment to register that he was about thirty and red-headed.

Clutching a towel round his waist, he clambered on to the top bench and stretched out flat. It was obvious that he wasn't wearing any swimming trunks and Carrie started to giggle. Francine seemed slightly annoyed at the newcomer's lack of modesty. She went out to the shower and came back smelling of shampoo.

Suddenly the red-headed man said, "Do any of you object to olbas oil?"

Carrie and I were lost so we didn't say anything. Francine said she liked it even if it was against the rules to use it. He clambered down clutching his scanty towel and managed to sprinkle some oil from a phial into a ladle of water.

"There's eucalyptus, pine, juniper, menthol . . . all sorts of oils," explained Francine.

The fumes enveloped us. It was like walking in a hot, moist forest.

"I think I've had enough time in here," said Francine. We took our cue from her and prepared to depart.

"Hold the door; I'm coming too," said Redhead. "I want an ice cold shower."

Carrie and I shuddered at the thought.

Francine pointed out the direction of the baths to us and went to the warm shower to wash off the conditioner. We delayed a moment in the rest area while Carrie tried to get her boots off.

"They've stretched," she said, "but not as much as my feet."

I volunteered to help her. We were standing by the cold shower and we could hear Redhead whistling behind the plastic curtain. We could see his feet, up to the hairy ankles in water.

Carrie sat on the edge of a recliner and I tugged at the first boot. As it came away, I said, "Loneliness must be having nobody to help you off with your boots."

"Hurry up, it's cold after being in there," replied Carrie.

I thought of leaving her with one boot on but then obligingly tugged at the second.

"You're pulling my foot off at the ankle," she complained.

At that moment, the boot came off. It spiralled out of my grasp, flew over the shower rail and attacked the occupant. He stopped whistling. The recliner tipped and Carrie shot headfirst through the shower curtain, landing in the icy water. I followed her quickly to help. There was Redhead, stark naked, covered in suds and Carrie's boot was frothing in the base of the shower.

*   *   *

Eventually we had a swim and that's when we had an unexpected meeting with Greg. I didn't recognise him at first. He bobbed up inches from my face with his hair slicked back by the water.

"I thought it was you," he said. "I saw this terrific bird

in this blue costume and I thought, 'I know her'."

"We've been in the sauna," I said as Carrie swam up to us.

"You should try it some time; it's very educational," she laughed. Greg looked curious but Carrie was swallowing too much water to continue so he turned back towards me.

"Don't ask!" I grinned. Carrie wasn't a very strong swimmer so she decided that discretion was the better part of valour and went off to spy out the talent in the shallow end.

"She gave you the lyrics?" I asked, feeling strangely reluctant to swim away.

"Yeah. We've made a terrific arrangement. Why don't you come to the shed to hear it?"

"Does Rick go to the shed often?" I asked, floundering physically and emotionally.

"Not much. I heard you two were an item."

"No, we're not, not any more," I said hastily, treading water and thinking this was the last place in the world to try to have a serious conversation. Greg was having difficulty staying afloat too. Somehow he seemed very vulnerable when he wasn't surrounded by the gear of the band.

"He wasn't right for you," Greg said as someone near us dived in the pool with a huge splash. We bobbed up and down for a moment in the wash of a wave and I knew that his comment was meant as consolation.

"I've missed you," he said. "When we were dancing at your party . . . "

Another wave interrupted the conversation and we drifted apart. We swam towards each other.

"Look," he said, as an underwater swimmer popped up between us, "I've got to dash. We've got a gig tonight and we have to get set up. I'll call you . . . "

As Carrie and I dried our hair in the foyer, the Asian gentleman was leaving the sauna and he greeted us.

"Oh hello," said Carrie. "You look different with your clothes on."

Carrie wore her trainers for the walk.

"Are you OK?" I asked.

"I've taken it in my stride," she grimaced. I always wondered whether she knew when she'd made a joke but I laughed out loud anyway.

"I'm glad somebody finds it funny," said Bobby, falling into step with us. "I told you this was a wellies job." He looked ruefully at the state of his splattered jeans.

"It's a real Slough of Despond," said Branwell, hurrying to join us.

"It's certainly muddy," I laughed and began to feel that life wasn't so bad after all.

Between us, with much laughter, we described our experience in the sauna.

"You mean, there were both men and women?" asked Branwell, visibly shocked.

"They'd be wearing their swimming gear," said Bobby.

"Not all of them," I laughed.

"Not as far as we could see," giggled Carrie. She continued with her graphic description.

"So there I am," she chortled eventually.

"One boot off and the other flying through the air," I continued, as part of our double act.

"You should have seen the guy's face," snorted Carrie.

"It wasn't his face we were looking at," I said and we both collapsed in a heap, laughing.

* * *

Sunday morning there was another letter waiting on the mat. It was very short.

"You harlot," it began. "I thought you were different from the rest, you painted Jezebel. A strumpet like you, masquerading as an angel of light, deserves all that befalls you." It was not signed but it was obviously from my previously "ardent admirer".

I couldn't understand my reaction to the letter. I felt I had let somebody down. I didn't know who was writing the letters but, strangely, I felt guilty as if I had betrayed him.

* * *

Carrie came round in the late afternoon. We had arranged to go to the evening service again.

Gloom had descended on Mum and Dad so Carrie and I took the hint and decided we would go to church by ourselves. By now I was sure she had nothing to do with the letters so I took her up to my room before we left and thrust the whole bundle into her hand.

"Nice paper," she said but as she carried on reading she made no further comments. Eventually she pushed the whole bundle to one side.

"They're kind of creepy, aren't they?" she said simply. "Have you really no idea who wrote them?"

"I've had lots of ideas," I said, hardly daring to look at her.

I had half expected her to leap on the puzzle with the enthusiasm of someone solving a whodunnit but she seemed to sense the tainted stench that the letters provoked. We sat on my bed in silence.

"I think we need some fresh air," she said at last.

"Yes, we don't want to be late," I said. "It's so embarrassing going into a service after it's started."

She picked up the letters as we left.

"You should put these in the dustbin," she said.

I looked doubtful. I felt bad about destroying them but I didn't know why.

"I'll see to it for you," she said. "This is the sort of things friends are for." I sensed she was telling me a very deep truth.

"They should be burnt on a ceremonial bonfire," she went on.

"There are rules about lighting fires," I laughed, remembering letters Dad had received from the local authorities for burning garden rubbish.

"Yes," Carrie agreed. "That's too good for them. They need to rot with old teabags and smelly potato peelings."

She took the letters round the side of our house to the dustbin and I felt strangely relieved.

* * *

A thought crossed my mind as I was listening to the sermon. The letters were destroyed but they had once existed. They couldn't be unwritten. I thought of a verse from a poem we had been studying at school:

> The moving finger writes
> And having writ
> Moves on.
> Not all thy piety nor wit
> Can lure it back
> To cancel half a line of it
> Nor all thy tears
> Wash out a word of it.

I closed my eyes and started thinking about coming to terms with the past and realised how the coursework about our visit to Coventry Cathedral had affected me. All my bad feelings about the letters would go in the bin with the potato peelings and the teabags. The writer was the one with the problem, not me. I would rise above it all, like a phoenix from the ashes, and, most important, I wouldn't hold any grudges. I was feeling quite smug till I felt Carrie nudging me. The jolt brought me back to earth. Oh dear, I hope the vicar didn't think I was going to sleep too, I thought, but Carrie wasn't trying to wake me up. She was trying to whisper something. I glared at her and tried to concentrate on the vicar

105

preaching about Christmas approaching soon. But Carrie couldn't wait to share her thought.

"If Jesus was born on the twenty-fifth of December," she whispered, "then He was a Capricorn." Carrie was heavily into fate, fortune and the stars.

I couldn't help smiling, anticipating the moment after the service when I would try to get her to tell Branwell this gem of an idea.

*   *   *

Bobby was amused by it but Branwell was shocked. Astrology was the work of the devil, in his opinion.

"I thought the three kings were following a star," insisted Carrie, never knowing when to leave well alone.

The comment threw Branwell. When nobody answered, Carrie turned to me for confirmation.

"Wasn't Jesus born under a wandering star?" she asked. That convulsed Bobby and me, knowing that she had a confused recollection of a song from an old film.

The vicar was doing his rounds and he paused to ask Bobby if he had ever thought of training for the ministry.

"We need healthy, upright young men who can be a role model for today's youth. I was very impressed with the way you conducted the sponsored walk and your rapport with the young people."

Bobby said he hadn't felt a vocation and suddenly remembered that he needed to go home early because his mother wasn't well. I could see from Carrie's eyes that she was thinking of how to angle Bobby into walking home with her on the way.

Branwell was earnestly telling the vicar that he was half considering the ministry himself as his future but the vicar didn't seem very impressed. I felt sorry for Branwell.

"Come on, Branwell," I said, "you can see me home. Carrie and Bobby won't have time to do a detour tonight."

Carrie smiled gratefully at me and rushed Bobby off before the plan could be changed.

Branwell stood his ground blinking resentfully at the world from behind his spectacles as the vicar said that I was in worthy hands, being escorted by Branwell, and hastened to wish us good night.

"Role models for today's youth," growled Branwell peevishly. "They've got enough like Bob in the church already."

I looked in the direction of the retreating forms of Carrie and Bobby. "Ah well; another thread in life's rich tapestry," I thought and couldn't help smiling.

"I thought Bobby was your friend," I said as Branwell rather ungraciously led me out of the church hall.

"He is," he replied sulkily.

"I know how it is," I said. "Carrie's my best friend but we're like chalk and cheese and sometimes I hate her."

"You're very like each other," he said. It didn't seem to be a compliment.

We walked in silence out into the dark lane leading towards my home. Or rather, I walked and he stomped.

I thought of telling him I'd go home by myself but I didn't like to see him looking so gloomy. Also I felt guilty at setting up the conversation about the stars which had so riled him, especially since now it felt like I'd been wanting a cheap laugh at his expense. He'd seemed depressed when he was singing in the choir so maybe there were other things on his mind and I'd made the situation worse.

"Lighten up," I said. "You're behaving as if the whole world has let you down."

"It has," he said abruptly. His stocky but powerful form bristled with pent-up emotion.

"Do you want to tell me about it?" I ventured.

"You? Tell you!"

That's when the penny dropped. There was so much venom in his voice.

"Oh my God," I whispered.

"Don't blaspheme," he snarled.

The trees shadowing the path seemed to be closing in on me. The moon had slid behind dark clouds and a night wind began to whisper threats. I quickened my pace but Branwell grasped my arm.

"Running from the truth?" he asked in a tone which was so level and so suddenly void of emotion that it turned my blood to ice.

"Don't be a victim; stand up to him," I thought.

"You're the one who can't face the truth," I said firmly. "I never gave you any reason to send me love letters."

He let go my arm and we confronted each other.

"Oh yes you did," he said. His bulk seemed to be growing and I unconsciously stretched to stand tall.

"When?" I demanded clearly. Panic still gripped me but I kept my breathing steady. I sensed that I must not let him scent my fear. I decided to take the initiative before he could answer and I changed my tone of voice.

"When, Branwell?" I asked evenly and impartially. "Tell me all about it. From the beginning."

It was as if he couldn't resist the opportunity to unburden his thoughts, even though I was the listener.

"I wasn't singing in the choir that night. I'd had tonsillitis and I was feeling very low." He paused and I knew I had to establish my control of the conversation.

"And then? What happened next, Branwell?"

He looked at me as if he wasn't sure where he was. I carefully stretched out my hand and took his arm, gradually moving us into a slow walk. He continued talking, almost in a dream.

"I looked round the church. I love that building. It looks different when you are sitting in the pews. Then I saw her. She . . . you . . . were sitting with your family. You were looking round too. I hadn't seen you in church for ages. You looked so pretty in your blue jacket and there was a window at the back. The light streamed through and the beams caressed your hair. You looked at me and I saw from your eyes that you recognised me. You smiled."

108

As I looked at him blinking seriously behind his glasses and seeming to shrink back to the familiar old friend I associated with Bobby, I felt compassion for him. I remembered that day and my polite smiles which covered the embarrassment I felt at returning to a place I had not attended for such a long time. I had forgotten I was wearing my blue jacket.

"Look, Branwell," I said as gently as I could, "you weren't in love with me. You had created somebody who wasn't real because you needed to love somebody." I could have been talking about my infatuation with Greg or with Rick but I resisted the urge to say that I knew what he was talking about because I had been there too. I knew I had to tread carefully or I would break the spell.

"You were in love with the idea of love. I just happened to be around."

When he didn't speak, I repeated the words.

"You were in love with love," I said, "because you are a sensitive, poetic, intelligent person."

When he still didn't speak, I thought I might have gone over the top but then I realised that he was listening attentively and waiting for more. I guessed it was because we were talking about his favourite subject – himself. Zeesham had been right. Quickly I moved the conversation forward.

"As for hating me, that was because I had spoilt your dream. I'm very sorry about that. But I'm sure that an intelligent person like you has great respect for the truth. You wouldn't want me to pretend." I was holding my breath now and very uncertain what to say next.

I felt like saying I had hated him too but I knew that some truths had to remain unspoken. I suddenly remembered how guilty I had felt when I read the last letter, as if in some way I had been responsible. Hesitantly, I continued, trying to keep my voice calm.

"Your letters were very beautiful. Why did you never sign your name?"

"Didn't you know they were from me?" His tone frightened me.

"Oh yes," I lied quickly, "I just wondered."

He seemed satisfied and I rushed into my next sentence.

"Thankyou for bringing me home, Branwell. I'm sorry I didn't match up to the sort of girl you wanted. But I'm sure you'll find one and I'm glad we've had this chance to sort things out. I'd like us to stay friends. I think we both need someone we can talk to honestly." As I said it, I knew I was telling the truth. He smiled at me.

"A platonic friendship," he said, "or, maybe, courtly love."

"What's that?" I asked apprehensively.

"Courtiers used to express their distanced admiration for their queen or the lady who gave them a favour, a handkerchief, to be her champion in the battle."

"That sounds fine to me," I laughed. "I'd better buy some handkerchiefs. I can't see you riding into battle with a box of tissues!"

* * *

As soon as I reached home, I told Mum all about it. Honestly and truthfully; every detail; every thought. I even went to the dustbin to retrieve the sodden letters. She was the perfect audience. She held her breath, frowned, puzzled, laughed and, in fact, lived the whole experience through my eyes.

"Unrequited love is terrible," she said eventually.

"It's worse being on the receiving end," I grimaced, "and it wasn't really love."

"So you know all about what is really 'love', do you?" she smiled.

"Do you?" I countered.

"I thought I did when I was your age," she laughed, "but I think you have advantages we didn't have."

I didn't ask about that; I simply asked again if she knew what love is.

"I can't explain it in words; but I can feel it. You were being very loving to Branwell tonight."

"Loving!" I exclaimed. "I was full of fear and hate."

"That's not the way it ended up," she said.

She stood up to wash our cups and to tidy the kitchen ready for breakfast.

"I believe," she said, "that in the future, people will have become so tired of chasing money that they will start chasing rainbows."

I couldn't believe these words were coming from my practical ordinary mother.

"What sort of rainbows?" I asked.

"The important things that bring colour into people's lives; their dreams; their hopes; their values."

I went up to bed to write a song about the future. Why had I never realised before that my mother was the source from which I had inherited the gift to think about life?

> History is not bunk
> Don't throw it out
> It's not junk
> > It holds the key
> > For you and me
> > To
> > The Future.
>
> Do you want wars on wars
> To carry on
> Scars on scars
> > Or take the key
> > For you and me
> > To
> > The Future?
>
> See a world full of need
> Cut your hatred
> Kill your greed

Here's the key
For you and me
To
The Future.

Someone means to offend
Catch his problem
Make him friend
There's the key
For you and me
To
The Future.

Do you want an answer
To cut out this
World's cancer?
Love's the key
For you and me
To
The Future.

4

"Valentine's Day is going to fall in half term," moaned Carrie.

She was counting the days in her diary till the next break from school.

"Yes, I know," I whispered with a cautious glance at our tutor who had asked us to be quiet while she totalled the register. Miss White closed the book with a flourish and a satisfied smile. The numbers must have added up for once. I continued speaking normally.

"I know it's at half term because that's when I'm going back to do some more work experience at the radio station. They've asked me to answer the phones for Love Lines – that's a programme going out live on Valentine's Day."

"You might have told me, Sarah."

"Do you want to answer the phones too?"

"No; you don't get paid. I meant that you didn't tell me it was in the holiday."

"I'm not a mind reader," I said.

"Valentine's Day is more fun when we're at school," she said, returning to her main grievance. "I was going to send Paleface a card."

"You didn't even send her a Christmas card," I remarked.

"Not from me; from Mr Lewisham."

"Valentines are supposed to be anonymous," said Zeesham from the desk behind us.

"I know that," sniffed Carrie, "but you have to be able to guess who sent it. Shane sent me one last year. It said 'To my ghoulfiend' and I knew it had to be from him."

113

"I didn't send you one!" protested Shane, who was sitting next to Zeesham.

"Oh yes, you did."

"Oh no, I didn't."

"Oh yes, you did," chanted the whole row.

"Oh no, he didn't," replied the other half of the class automatically in response.

"Oh no, not again," said Miss White with a tolerant sigh.

The class returned to their own conversations and Carrie stuck her tongue out at Shane but she was smiling. She would continue to think what she wanted to think. I kept quiet. I'd sent the card.

"How many valentines do you think you'll get?" Carrie asked me.

"You make it sound like counting scalps. You can put notches on your hockey stick."

"I can't stand hockey," she said.

"The real question is," I continued, "how many are you going to SEND?"

"I'm going to send one to my dad," said Carrie, then seemed to regret having spoken her idea out loud. She rushed on. "I wonder if Branwell will send you one from your ardent admirer?"

"That's a sick joke," I complained but I smiled all the same and reflected on the way time healed bad memories. It had been less than two months ago that Rick and I had split up and Branwell had been pestering me with love letters. We'd seen a lot of Branwell and Bobby at the Christmas activities in church and had remained friendly, though Carrie's hoped-for romance with Bobby had not materialised.

"Should we send one to Branwell for a laugh?" asked Carrie. "A real sexy one."

"No way!" I said hastily. "He might take it seriously!"

"No prizes for guessing who Paul and Samantha are sending cards to," grinned Carrie looking round the room speculatively.

"I'd get bored to death if I was one of those two," I said looking across at the lovebirds. "They hang around together so much, you'd think they were joined at the hip."

"Who are you going to send one to?" Carrie asked.

I shrugged in answer. I'd nobody to send a valentine to and I felt sad. I'd seen Greg a few times but we were both careful not to make any commitment and I had the distinct feeling that he was learning from past mistakes too. Despite our cautiousness, we were becoming genuine friends and, of course, the songs were a common interest. But I felt that sending a valentine would be a bad move.

"We could send one to Bobby," Carrie said. She paused and her eyes lit up with mischief. "Better still, we could send one from Bobby to Branwell!"

"That's definitely not funny," I snapped.

"I suppose you're right. You have to be careful with a nutter like Branwell. He's all right though," she commented amiably.

"And what's all this about 'us' sending cards," I asked rather loudly and suddenly became conscious that the rest of the room was very quiet.

"Sarah," said Miss White, "you're getting as bad as Caroline. You haven't noticed me standing here. I'm ready now to start our tutor group assembly."

I blushed and Carrie rushed to my defence.

"We were only saying that Valentine's Day is at half term." The tutor group groaned with disappointment at this news.

"I'm sure that fact is of paramount importance and can't wait till after prayers," said Miss White drily but Carrie missed the irony.

"Too right, miss," she answered and it was clear from the ribald comments flying around the room that the rest of the class agreed with her.

Miss White gave an exasperated sigh but retained her cool. She smiled and said how appropriate it was that we were thinking of Valentine's Day because the reading she had chosen from was from I Corinthians 13 which was known as the Hymn to Love.

"What him is that, miss?" asked Carrie raising her hand.

"Caroline, how many times do I have to tell you that I'm pleased you remember to put up your hand but you must wait to speak. Otherwise, you are just shouting out."

"Well, I only wanted to know who he was," muttered Carrie sulkily, without even putting her hand up.

"He?" asked Miss White, perplexed, giving up on her attempt to instil classroom etiquette.

"The Him to love."

We all groaned and Miss White's habitual smile was looking strained.

"The Song in praise of Love," she amended and went on to explain that, unlike us, the Greeks didn't have just one word which had to cover many different things. They had at least four words for love.

"First there is 'storge' which means 'liking'. I like rice pudding."

Carrie wrinkled her nose; she hates rice pudding.

Miss White hurried on before there could be any interruptions. "Perhaps it's better to say it means 'affection', as in 'I like my cat'." The class tolerated this explanation.

"Then there is the word 'eros', which is erotic sexual love." All the class sat up and started to pay attention.

"Then there is 'philos' – love of your family and friends. But the word used in this chapter is not storge, not eros, not philos but 'agape'. It used to be translated into English as charity but that word has come to mean something different nowadays. Agape is all the other loves rolled into one. It is perfect love. It is God's love to us and shining through us to other people."

She explained that in the passage she was going to read, Paul was writing a letter to Christians at Corinth.

"They remind me of you lot sometimes; they had hearts of gold but they could be very quarrelsome. So

116

Paul reminds them what real love is like . . . "

She began to read.

"Love is patient and kind; love is not jealous or boastful; it is not arrogant or rude. Love does not insist on its own way; it is not irritable or resentful . . . "

As I listened I decided that I would go home and read the whole chapter; maybe the whole book.

"You know," concluded Miss White, "Paul thought that love was more important than faith and hope."

"Well, that's obvious," said Carrie and Miss White didn't bother to tell her that she hadn't put up her hand.

We had a moment's quiet at the end instead of a prayer and we were supposed to be thinking about how real love means putting other people first. I don't know what Carrie's thoughts were about but straight afterwards she said to me, "I don't suppose we could have another party for Valentine's Day?"

"I didn't think you were into hearts and flowers," I said.

"No!" she exclaimed. "A Valentine's Day Massacre Party. I'd love to dress up as a gangster's moll!"

*   *   *

We didn't have a party and, as far as cards were concerned, Valentine's Day was a total non-event for us. Carrie hadn't got round to sending any, apart from the one to her dad, and though she told me she had received two valentines I didn't believe her because I had said that I had received two cards as well. Neither of us showed any inclination to display the cards to each other.

"They're supposed to be anonymous," said Carrie when we met up at lunchtime in the coffee bar and I was happy to leave it at that.

When I had seen the lack of post on the doormat that morning, I felt sad. I told myself that receiving no letters is better than receiving unwanted letters but it wasn't much consolation. The fact remained that I had no one special in my life. Answering the phone at the radio station had rubbed the fact in.

"You should have heard them," I said to Carrie. "It was enough to make you sick."

"I know," she agreed. "We had the radio on in the shoe shop."

"Plum Pud loves Apple Dumpling," I mimicked, "and Squidgey Widgey is missing Cuddly Wuddly Bear!"

"The only thing they're missing is their brains," sniffed Carrie.

"It's all a hype, all this Valentine's Day lark. It's got nothing to do with real love," I complained.

"Too right," said Carrie. "It's worse than Christmas. Just another excuse to make money." We were egging each other on in expressing our resentment. I suppose we were both feeling disappointed but neither of us was prepared to admit it.

"As if you can put a price tag on love," I said. "And it puts pressure on people," I went on. "Take my mum and dad. They don't send each other a card because they think it's a waste of money. They put the same two cards up each year. But he still feels obliged to buy her a bunch of roses."

"They're expensive in February," commented Carrie.

"Yes, Dad always says that."

We nursed our coffee cups and stared out of the window. There seemed to be couples everywhere I looked.

"My mum will be in a real state tonight," said Carrie. "She gets sentimental. She'll have all the old photos out and then she'll start crying.

"I hope my dad got the card I sent," she added as an afterthought.

"What sort of card was it?" I asked curiously. She'd said that she hated him so much when he left home that I thought she might have sent one of those really abusive valentines.

"It wasn't cheap," she said, "it had a satin heart and lace."

"Did you sign it?" I asked.

"Of course not," she replied, "but he'll know it's from me."

"How's life in the shoe trade?" I asked to change the subject. Carrie scowled. The boss in the shop seemed to have taken over as the main subject of her grudges. According to Carrie, he had unreasonable expectations about politeness and punctuality.

"How's the radio station?" she asked eventually when she had exhausted her list of complaints about the shoe shop.

"Answering the phones on Valentine's Day is the pits," I said with a laugh, "but this afternoon they're going to show me how to do a vox pop and then I'm back on the phones again, just for an hour at teatime."

"What's a vox pop?" Carrie asked.

"Just interviewing people in the street."

"Well it beats fitting shoes on their smelly feet."

*   *   *

Just over an hour later I was standing in the middle of a park near the radio station with a microphone in one hand, a heavy tape recorder hanging from the other shoulder and very apprehensive butterflies shivering in my gut.

I was trying not to look nervous because that was rule number one but my head was buzzing with the rest of the tips I had been given in my five-minute training session before I left the radio station.

"Wrap the lead round your hand or you'll get a rattle from the flex. Listen carefully to the letters P and B to make sure you don't get a popping noise. Don't leave the machine on when you're not interviewing . . ."

I had managed to find a small group of children who were willing to talk to me.

"No, you're not a pop singer," I said to a little black girl called Esther. "Don't try to grab the microphone."

I disentangled the flex from the pretty ribbons in her hair.

"I'll hold it here in the centre and you all gather round so that I can take a level of the sound of your voices."

Wide-eyed and giggling the children jostled round me.

"No, not round the tape machine – round the microphone."

Anxiously I arranged them so that the ones with the lightest voices were nearer to the mike.

As I did so, I was recalling the instructions the producer had given.

"All I want you to do is get some material for an 'Ah!' spot. That's where the listeners hear twee little comments by kids and go, 'Aaah! Isn't that sweet'."

"What a cynic," I had thought but I told him I was interested in the challenge of getting good radio material and yet keeping true to the spirit of the interviewees.

"Just my luck, to choose a reporter with integrity," he groaned but I sensed his approval.

The children's comments were going to be used as an introduction to the teatime valentine phone-in.

"Have you ever been kissed?" I asked Esther. She held the edge of her skirt with one hand and put her other hand over her face and squirmed with embarrassment.

"It's yucky!" volunteered a freckled fat boy.

"Say that as a sentence. Kissing is . . . " I prompted.

"Kissing is yucky, yucky, yucky," he said obligingly.

I delayed before asking my next question because I knew my voice would be cut out and I wanted to make the editing easy.

"Today is a special day. Do you know what day it is?"

Esther had found her voice.

"It's my birthday," she lisped.

"What a lucky girl," I said, automatically putting the machine on pause. They all started talking at once about their birthdays.

By some miracle, I completed the assignment. I knew the material was good and I was especially pleased with the final comment.

"You shouldn't kiss a boy with braces," said Esther. "'Cos if you've got braces on your teeth and he's got braces on his teeth, you get locked together." Then she collapsed with giggles and managed to breathe, "I know, 'cos it happened to me!"

*   *   *

The producer, Max, was pleased with the tape. I watched him edit with lightning speed and when I was seated at the phones I flicked the switch to enable me to hear the finished product being transmitted. An afternoon's work was over in two minutes, but it was good quality. I settled to pay attention to my task but, as I was about to switch off the transmission, I heard Max say that he had a studio guest, the lead singer from a local group called Brilliant Corners. The song was "Love is the Future". I swivelled to look through the glass to the studio we called the "goldfish bowl". Sure enough, there was Greg, with earphones on, seated at a table in front of a microphone, nervously listening to the record and waiting for the cue to speak. So the group had changed its name again and they were singing one of my songs. Greg looked towards the window and recognised me. He grinned and gave a thumbs-up signal. As the last chord died away, Max was already halfway through his first question.

"Before I ask you anything else, have you a message for anyone?"

"Yes," replied Greg. "For the girl who wrote the lyrics. Happy Valentine's Day, Sarah. Incidentally, I'm no longer a pre-packaged Romeo."

*   *   *

Greg waved as he left the studio and I carried on taking

the phone calls with a much lighter heart. The requests didn't seem silly any more. The time passed quickly and I found I was enjoying myself. Then a curious thing happened as we were coming to the end of the show.

"Hello," I said into the telephone, "this is your family radio station, Livewire Central. Name, please, and telephone number."

"I want to give a message to a girl called Samantha."

"Name please."

"Samantha. I just told you."

"YOUR name, please."

"Paul," the agitated voice went on. "Just tell her I still love her even if they won't let me see her."

"Your telephone number?"

"I don't want to talk to the DJ. Just give out the message. PLEASE." The line went dead.

I looked thoughtfully at the words I had scribbled. I was sure I had recognised the voice and I was surprised that Paul had not recognised mine. My impersonation of an efficient radio secretary must have been better than I imagined. Then I remembered that Paul had been away from school the previous fortnight so probably he didn't know I was working on the phones.

"So, things aren't working out for the lovebirds," I thought as I got up to take my sheaf of requests to the studio. Waiting for the red light over the adjoining door to change to green, I remembered that Samantha had been away from school too.

"Strange how they always catch each other's colds," Carrie had commented drily.

*   *   *

"This one just wants a message read over the air," I said to Max, who was presenting as well as producing the show. I gave the paper directly to him rather than leaving it on the waiting pile. He took it and, while he concentrated on working the desk with his other hand, he waved the paper about, apparently indicating that I should wait a moment. The romantic music was growing imperceptibly quieter as Max moved the fader connected to the deck and slickly opened the one which controlled his microphone. The red light on the wall above the desk winked into action and I kept very still and silent.

Max spoke over the background tune, caressing the microphone with his voice.

"Music for lovers. And guess who called to say he loves YOU, Samantha? If true love is not running smoothly for you, sweetheart, always remember that PAUL – though he cannot be with you – loves you from the bottom of his heart. Sweet daydreams, Samantha, sunshine, as you listen to a song that has become a classic . . . "

I watched, fascinated by his dexterity as his fingers drew the faders in opposite directions so one tune was gradually eclipsed by another and as he briskly cut his microphone. The red light went dead. I was even more impressed by the casual manner in which he held a conversation with me even though he knew he had only three minutes before the end of the record and there were still other things he had to do. As he talked he was watching the dial that indicated the station was still on the air and listening on a pre-fade to the level of sound of the next disc which he had placed on the deck.

"To check that I won't blow their eardrums out," he explained automatically and went straight on with what he wanted to tell me. "You've done well today, Sarah. I'm planning a series for the summer. It's called the Generation Gap. I want you to find a few teenagers, including yourself. I'm going to interview them and their parents, separately, about various topics. Then I'm going to splice their answers and put them together to see if there really is a generation gap."

I nodded enthusiastically.

Max glanced at the revolving record, estimated the available time, took a sheet of paper from the pile I had brought and picked up the phone. He cradled the receiver in the crook of his neck as he dialled and smiled at me.

"I liked your song," he said. His tone changed to that of the jokey presenter: "Hello, caller. This is your lucky Valentine's Day. Are you ready to give me your message? Now, listen carefully. Don't hang up; just put the receiver down while you turn off your radio. Then come straight back to the phone and wait for me to ask your name. Got it? Fine." As he spoke he was checking the pre-fade linked to the line which would bring in the caller's voice, then he pressed a button and a small machine made the sound of a telephone bell. Max's hands were busy pushing faders and flicking switches. I watched in awe.

"Hello, caller – welcome to Valentine Special on your friendly family radio station, Livewire Central. What's your name? . . . "

The red light was on so I had to wait till he'd finished.

As I turned to go, Max said, "I'll be in touch. It will be after your exams."

* * *

The phone was ringing as I walked into our house.

"That will be Carrie. She's rung twice already," said Mum, as she arranged some red roses in a bowl.

"Those are pretty," I said as I picked up the receiver. Mum smiled with pleasure.

"At last!" Carrie screeched down the phone. "I thought you were never coming home. I've something to tell you."

"Down the café in an hour," I said out of habit, "I'll have to have my tea first."

"No," said Carrie, "I'm staying in tonight. But I just had to ring you."

It was obvious that she couldn't wait to tell me her news. She launched straight into the tale.

"You remember I sent a card to my dad? An anonymous one. Well, his new bird thought he'd been two-timing her. She threw a wobbly. All the jealousy stuff.

They had a real set-to and . . . she threw him out. He's back home!"

"That's great news!" I said. "Isn't it?" I was cautious because you never really knew how things stood with Carrie's family.

"Yes! Yes!" she said jubilantly. "Mum had got all sentimental because it was Valentine's Day, like I knew she would. She'd got all the photos out and that's when he came home. We're going to be a real family again."

With the last sentence, her tone had changed. She sounded almost wistful.

"It's going to be all right, isn't it?" she said.

"Of course it is," I reassured her.

I'd only just put the phone down when it began to ring again. I thought it was going to be Carrie but it was Greg.

"How do you fancy coming down the shed? You haven't been to one of our rehearsals in a long time. We're celebrating our success."

"Take your key if you're going out," said Mum, walking through from the kitchen with an apple pie – Dad's favourite.

"There's no such thing as a private phone call in this house," I grumbled but I was smiling. "I'm going to see Greg."

"That's nice," said Mum.

As I went to join my parents at the table, ready to tell them about the radio station, I reflected on the change there had been in our relationship over the past year.

As I sat down I said, "Happy Valentine's Day."

*　　*　　*

It was Monday and we were back in school.

"How are things at home?" I asked Carrie.

"Going well so far. But I'm keeping my fingers crossed," she said. "You know how it is with my family. I can hardly believe myself that it's true; that it will last."

125

We looked at our timetables but made very little effort to get ready for the first lesson.

"I think they married too young," said Carrie.

"I think mine waited too long. They were in their thirties," I said.

"Ugh! That's ancient. Now they're getting back together," said Carrie, reverting to the topic of her parents, "they'll have to work at it."

"Well, that's what real love is," I agreed. "It's not an airy-fairy feeling. You've got to live it. Then it grows into real love."

"I've been thinking," Carrie said. "I don't want to wait till I'm old but I don't want to be like Nita."

I was surprised. Nita had been her heroine lately.

"What's wrong with Nita?"

"Well, who wants to work in that shoe shop till they find 'Mister Right'? If she hadn't found that bloke of hers, that chiropodist, where would she be?"

"So?" I asked.

"Well, I've been thinking about staying on at school or going to college. I know it's only a short half-term till Easter and the exams come soon after that but, if you'll help me get down to it, I'm going to revise really hard . . ."

* * *

Carrie's resolution had a few setbacks that morning because she hadn't done any homework.

"Teachers don't give you a chance," she complained at lunchtime. "They don't believe I've turned over a new leaf."

"Give them time," I said, "you've only been reformed for one morning."

A group of little first years walked past us. None of them seemed to have grown into the clothes which their parents had bought to last a long time and their bags were nearly as big as they were.

126

"Wouldn't it be nice to be like that still," said Carrie watching their progress across the yard. "No coursework, no worries," she sighed. We sat in silence in our favourite spot, staring into space; both trying to grasp a glimpse of the future.

Miss White was on lunch duty. She was looking pre-occupied, as if something was on her mind, but she paused to greet us.

"I'm thinking of staying on at school," Carrie blurted out. Miss White looked startled and I smiled. It was the first time I'd seen our tutor totally thrown by anything we said.

"I thought you had a job lined up at a shoe shop," said Miss White. "I wrote your reference."

"Not everybody wants to marry a chiropodist," said Carrie.

Miss White looked even more non-plussed.

"Well, yes. I can see that point of view," she said, not seeing at all.

"The girl she was replacing is marrying a chiropodist," I said helpfully.

"Well, I hope they'll be very happy," said Miss White, stalling for time and sense in the conversation. "Are you telling me you want to stay on at school, Carrie?"

"I just said."

"You're not just deciding this because Sarah is staying on, are you?" asked Miss White smiling apologetically in my direction.

"No. I just think education is a good thing. I'm a reformed character."

"Well, I'm glad you feel like that and I'm sure your teachers will be pleased."

Somehow her voice lacked conviction. She must have guessed that some teachers were counting the days till Carrie left.

*　　*　　*

"I don't think she believes me," grumbled Carrie during afternoon registration.

"It's just that it takes some getting used to," I said, looking round the room. Something else was on my mind. "I've just realised that Paul and Sam are still not back," I said.

Risking getting told off for talking when the register was being called, I whispered to Carrie about Paul's phone call to the radio.

"I forgot all about it, what with the news about your dad and everything else . . . "

"Everything else?" she queried.

I hesitated. I always felt uncomfortable talking to Carrie about Greg.

"After you rang, Greg called and I saw him that night. It might be starting up again between us; except I don't want to get involved with anybody at the moment, not with exams and all that."

"Yes, we've got to think about the future," said Carrie loudly with the enthusiasm of a new convert.

"The reformation didn't last very long, did it?" said Miss White and Carrie lapsed into a sulk which lasted all afternoon.

*　　*　　*

"Isn't that Paul?"

"Talk of the devil . . . " I said.

Carrie and I were on our way home. We were taking a short cut through the grounds of the hospital.

"It is, isn't it?" She was just about to wave and yell in characteristic Carrie fashion when an instinct made me stop her.

We drew back behind a parked car and observed him. He was dawdling outside the main door of one of the buildings, smoking a cigarette. His manner seemed very distracted and indecisive. He looked as if he wanted to go into the building. Suddenly he threw down the smouldering butt and ground the cigarette beneath the sole of his boot. Stuffing his hands into his pockets and with his shoulders hunched, he took one more look at the building then turned and strode towards the main road.

"Perhaps we ought to go after him," I said.

"No, I think you were right not to let him see us. What do you think is going on?" I didn't answer but I suppose we were both already beginning to guess what had happened. I looked round as if for inspiration. Carrie was doing the same.

"Hey, look! Isn't that Miss White's car?" We went over to peer in the car window and some coursework on the back seat confirmed that Carrie was right.

"We're going inside," I said, turning resolutely towards the building.

*   *   *

There was a reception desk just inside the door but the woman behind it looked very formidable. I took Carrie's arm and wheeled her round, leading her back outside.

"I thought we were going in," she said.

"Yes, but I've got a better idea. Wasn't there a public call box by the car park?"

We squashed into the phone booth and I asked Directory Enquiries for the number of the hospital.

"Hello. General Hospital? I believe you have a Miss Samantha Poole; I'd like to know the number of the ward to send the get well card to."

*   *   *

We walked as confidently as possible through the hospital doors, without looking at the lady on the reception desk, and followed the signs along the corridor and up the stairs to the ward where we had been told Sam would be.

"Leave it to me," I instructed Carrie as we entered

129

through the swing doors. I approached a young nurse in the area which led to the beds. "We're waiting for our teacher," I said. "She's with Samantha Poole."

"They're in the second cubicle on the right – the one with the curtain drawn round it – but I don't think Sam is ready for visitors . . . "

"It's all right. We understand. We'll wait here. Thankyou."

She pointed to two chairs and left us. When the coast was clear we stood and moved to stand by the curtain.

There was a gap and we could see Sam and Miss White. It was the sort of scene which etches itself on your memory. Samantha was sobbing and Miss White had her arms around her.

"I know you think I've been stupid. But we didn't mean it to happen. And I do love him. And I was rude to you when you tried to talk to me . . . "

"Now, now," murmured Miss White, seeming to be as vulnerable as Samantha and very unsure of herself. "Now, now, forget all that."

Samantha was swaying in Miss White's embrace and trying to force words through a torrent of grief.

"Just tell me; tell me the truth; nobody tells me the truth; nobody tells me anything; just tell me," wailed Sam. "They don't, do they? They don't put them in dustbins, do they? I read it. I read it in a magazine. They don't, do they?"

The scene will stay with me for ever. I had called a song "Love in a Dustbin" when I had simply been thinking about throwing away the images people had about love. Now my friend was facing her experience of love and its consequences. My concerns of the past year seemed petty and trivial by comparison. She had given a whole new meaning to the words which had slipped so glibly from my tongue.

Miss White patted Sam's shoulder as they clung to each other.

"No, no, Sam; believe me, they don't. They don't put

them in dustbins. Honestly, they don't." She stroked Sam's hair and struggled to find words with the hopelessness of someone who knows that there is nothing to say. "You've got to put the whole experience behind you now."

Miss White in her grief turned her head to rest on Samantha's arm and that was when she realised we were there. Gently she extricated herself from the embrace and told Sam to rest.

"Try to get some sleep," she said, blinking back tears. "Your parents will come back this evening."

"I don't want them to come back!"

"No, hush. They care about you. Try to understand how they feel. And remember, we all care about you. I know Paul cares about you. Now hush. Try to sleep. Things will get better. I promise."

* * *

Miss White didn't confront us with questions. She merely placed her arms around our shoulders and shepherded us out of the building.

"Did she have an abortion?" asked Carrie bluntly as we stood in the car park.

"No. Fortunately that decision didn't have to be made. She ... well, she was so upset ... she had a natural miscarriage."

Miss White looked as if she was weighing her words.

I said hastily, "We won't say anything, will we, Carrie?"

"No, we won't," Carrie stated and I knew she meant it.

"We saw Paul," she told Miss White. "He was hanging around outside. He didn't see us but he walked off that way."

As she pointed, I realised once again that sometimes Carrie was quicker than I was at seeing what mattered. Paul must be going through hell too.

131

"That's a useful piece of information," said Miss White. "I'll try to catch up with him. Maybe I can arrange for him to visit before her parents return."

"They don't want him to visit, do they?" I stated flatly.

"No. But everybody needs some time now to cope with their feelings. Things will get better," she said.

"She's in a difficult position," I said as we watched the car speed away.

"Not half as difficult as Sam," said Carrie as we morosely continued our journey home. "I know how she feels."

I plodded along and nodded in agreement.

"But I really do," said Carrie. "I really do. It could have been me. I thought I was in the same boat once. But I was lucky."

"When?" As the word came out of my mouth I knew I ought to stop her telling me. It was too late. She had to tell me and I knew that we had both been waiting for this moment for a long time.

"There's something I have to tell you," said Carrie. "It goes back to last autumn. One night you went to catch the last bus and I . . . well, Greg and I . . . well, that night you left me with Greg . . . "

My mind boggled. I'd known yet I hadn't known. I'd shut myself off from what had really happened. Part of me wanted to force her to put it into words but I said, "It's all right, Carrie, I know."

She wasn't listening. She was intent on telling me and she persevered.

"You went to catch the bus," she said as if I needed to be told the sequence of events. Yet I could remember them as if they were yesterday. I said nothing.

"I suppose I was flattered." Carrie wasn't telling me; she was simply speaking out loud.

"And," she added miserably, "I think I was getting one over on you. Don't ask me why. I don't even understand it myself.

"Do you remember when I gave you such a hard time

132

after the birthday party," she continued, "because you had a date with Rick? I think that was all tied up with feeling guilty about that night with Greg. I wanted to feel I was justified somehow." She paused and I knew she was going back in time.

"That night with Greg; I didn't know how to go about saying no." Was it that I didn't want to hear or was I simply trying to help her when I interrupted? I wasn't sure of my motives.

"I know about you and Greg." She didn't seem to be hearing me so I repeated it. "It's all right, Carrie. I know. I guessed what was going to happen and the next day I just knew."

She went crimson. She was hearing me at last.

"You mean you've known all the time?"

She moaned with a sound that you cannot describe but only feel. It cut me to the bone.

"All this time. You've known?"

"Yes."

"Didn't you hate me?"

"Yes. At first. You'll never know how much I hated you. It wasn't Greg. I didn't care about him. It was because I thought you were my friend. That's what hurt me."

"Oh, you're making me feel rotten. All those weeks, all those months, you've known . . ."

I was beginning to wish I'd not told her that I knew but it was too late now. Her shoulders were hunched and tears were trickling down her cheeks.

"It's not the times we were fighting," she said, "it was the good times. They weren't real, were they? All the time you knew."

More and more I wished I had not told her the truth. I felt as if I had stolen something precious from her.

"So all the time you were pretending to be my friend."

"I was your friend; I AM your friend."

"No, you couldn't have been. I can't bear it; the fact that you knew."

133

"What difference does it make?"

"It's like you've stolen from me." Suddenly it was like talking to Branwell again.

"Stolen?" I said.

"All the things I remember. The good things. You knew all the time. You must have been hating me – when I thought you were my friend."

"But . . . the good times were real," I said, "I got over it. Honestly, it doesn't matter."

"It does. It does matter. I betrayed you and you are the only friend I have. You are the only person who matters to me."

"But . . . " I began. Suddenly all the buts I could say would have no meaning.

"You knew. All the time you knew."

"Yes, but it wasn't important. We're still friends. That's what matters. We've come through it and we're still friends."

It was hard to get the next words through my lips. They weren't the words one girl says to another.

"I love you, Carrie."

In the moment that I said to Carrie that I loved her, I understood that you can't weigh, measure or define love. No words would ever tell her. I put my arms around her.

"I love you, Carrie," I repeated.

All her hysteria collapsed. She clung to me.

"I love you too, Sarah."

She wiped the tears into a streak across her face and tried to grin.

"It's a good job nobody is listening to us or they'd get some funny ideas."

"Yes; it's sad, isn't it," I said, "that you can't tell your friends that you love them without explaining what you mean."

"I know," she said.

We stood in silence for a while but the atmosphere was good, as if every second was healing the hurt we had caused each other. The silence was better than words because the meaning of our thoughts was clear.

* * *

I looked round the hall. The weeks had flown past. This would be the last end-of-term service for us because the next term we would be absent after the examinations.

The headmaster stood centre stage and looked down at us over his glasses.

"As principal of this school," he said, "I wear many hats."

I saw the first years looking at him solemnly. Some were obviously puzzled because he wasn't wearing even one hat. He had nothing on his head; not even much hair.

"Some of my tasks are onerous."

Gazing at the uncomprehending faces, he realised that he had drawn a blank. He tried again.

"Sometimes I have the unpleasant task of reminding you about litter and your behaviour on the buses."

From the shuffling and coughing it was clear that everyone had understood him this time.

"Today, however, it is my pleasure to wish you a happy Easter vacation. Mind how you go on the roads. And now we'll sing our hymn which Miss White tells me is written by Sarah Simpson. It is entitled 'Mandatum novum da vobis', which is our school motto. That, as you know, means 'A new commandment I give you'."

He paused to glare at someone in the front row then nodded towards the music master.

My heart sank. I thought the introduction would kill the atmosphere. The music master must have shared my opinion. Before starting to play, he said, "The new commandment is that you should love one another. I'm very pleased with Sarah's hymn and I think you will find it easy to sing. It's a very exciting experience being the first people to try out something new. I'll play it through once so you can get the hang of it."

135

An overhead projector screen was splaying the words behind the piano and Miss White moved over to the projector so she could point to the words in time to the music. Greg had written the sort of tune which would work well at a football match. It was a community "sway and sing". The whole school picked up the tune quickly but I sensed it was because our tutor group were singing their guts out. I glanced along the lines of familiar faces and I caught Miss White also looking along the rows with a proud smile.

I remembered the bickering mob we had been when the year had begun. Shane was chewing gum but he swallowed it with a gulp when he saw Miss White raise an eyebrow. Samantha and Paul were standing together. I felt a wave of affection flow from me towards them and sadly accepted that I would never be able to offer them my sympathy. Carrie and I had kept our promise to Miss White. We had never let on to Sam and Paul or to anyone else that we knew what had happened, though Carrie and I discussed it sometimes.

"You can't call your song 'Love in a Dustbin' any more," Carrie said. I knew she was right. So, "Love and Trash" it remained.

Carrie was standing next to me in the assembly. Zeesham was on the other side. He nudged me as the singing came to an end and turned to whisper his congratulations.

The headmaster was speaking again. He obviously felt we needed a sermon before the holidays.

He looked over his glasses at the wide-eyed first years grouped in the front rows, craning their necks, and he addressed most of his remarks to them.

"Love is more important than faith and hope," he said. "There are situations in life when faith and hope become unnecessary – for trust has been fulfilled and dreams have been realised . . . "

He looked round the room to make sure that we had all appreciated his poetic phrasing.